Ysgol Gynradd Llanwrda
Llanwrda
Sir Gaeryrddin
SA19 8L4D
Rhif Ffôn: 01550 777552

# FINDING MINERVA

Frances Thomas

Published in 2007 by Pont Books, an imprint of
Gomer Press, Llandysul, Ceredigion, SA44 4JL

ISBN 9781843237464

A CIP record for this title is available from the British Library.
© Copyright: Frances Thomas, 2007

The author asserts her moral right under the
Copyright, Designs and Patents Act, 1988
to be identified as author of this work.

This book is published with the financial support of the
Welsh Books Council.

Printed and bound in Wales at
Gomer Press, Llandysul, Ceredigion

# 1

Afterwards, she'd remember that day as the last one when she could walk through the streets without having to worry about who was following her, or who might be lurking in dark alleyways; the last day without being afraid . . .

Normal life changed utterly that evening in early November.

It was getting late as Livia left her violin teacher's house and the sky was darkening to soft violets and purples and greys. Mrs Rees had dithered and fussed, someone had come to the door with a message, and her pet dog knocked a cup of tea from the table, so that the lesson didn't start until nearly half an hour late – and then Mrs Rees got on to the subject of her daughter's wedding and brought out the photographs. Livvy thought it would be unkind to mention the curfew so she listened politely. If she hurried, she should get home in plenty of time.

Mrs Rees lived in the far suburbs in a quiet street of red-brick houses shaded with plum and cherry trees. The air smelled of woodsmoke and wet earth. Beyond her house were allotments, and beyond those, endless flat wheatfields stretched away to the dusky bulge of the Wrekin. In the distance you could hear the slow melancholy boom of the steam barges on the canal.

Livvy liked it out here in the quiet streets beyond the hustle of the city. Often when they were younger, she and Max would pack bread, cheese and apples, and come down here to sit by the canal and watch the quiet solemnities of trade, the comings and goings of the heavy barges, the loading and unloading, the men shouting and cursing, their great muscled and tattooed shoulders glistening with sweat. Neither of their mothers of course knew they travelled so far, imagining them to be safely in the children's playpark with the baby goats and the swings. But they shared, both of them, an urge to go beyond the safe and familiar. And as long as brother Tony wasn't around, Livvy could get away with it.

But now, as she rounded the street corner, violin-case in hand, in her calf-length woollen dress, her winter coat, long brushed hair tucked under a dark red beret, she looked demure enough, a young Roman-British girl going safely home to her hearth.

A tram was just pulling slowly away, with a whine and a gasp of steam, and though she probably could have caught it if she ran, she let it go.

She walked quickly, down the broad street that led to the city centre. Shop owners were closing up, pulling down shutters and locking grilles. People were so much more careful since the riots – though she could hardly remember the time before; they spoke of being able to leave doors unlocked, and of neighbourhood shops staying open late into the evening. Now, except for the centre where nightclubs, theatres and restaurants still flourished on non-curfew evenings, the city was like a ghost town at night.

She left the main road, and the streets became narrower and the tenements higher and grimmer, massing above her now with their dark stinking stairwells, their broken windows, their barking, tethered dogs. Something clattered at her feet, and she turned to see a gang of young men lounging in a doorway, defying the near-curfew hour. Thin and dark-eyed and dangerous, with their tattooed brows and wrists, they were fascinating in a way she wasn't supposed to notice, and though she turned her head demurely away when they called 'Hey, you, *cariad,* join us in a drink, won't you?' part of her wanted to do so rather than spend the evening playing languid backgammon with Mother.

She turned left just before she got to Forum Square and took a narrow back street. Tony would have had a heart attack if he knew she was taking this short cut.

Another turn into a narrow muddy lane between high stone walls smelling of urine and rubbish. Then a sharp dash across a building site.

Then she was in the Temple Quarter.

She hated it here, especially in the dark, the eerie cobbled square and the temples: some ornate in the ancient style with porticos and steps, Isis, Minerva, Vesta, Mars; some, like those of the Christians, simple and bleak. The big Jupiter temple was shuttered and nearly derelict now, though sometimes a few ancient priests tottered in and out. More scary – and much more popular in these days of political unease – were the old Cymric Gods: Sulis and Bran and Artor and Rhiannon, who lurked behind high walls and shuttered gates where there were ancient sacred trees, and dark fountains fed, so it was said, on blood.

Only the Mithraic temples – her brother's beloved Mithras – had managed to evade the zoning policy that massed all the other temples together. Their ancient, cherished secretive little temples lurked all over the city, as watchful and silent and alert as the Military Police themselves.

Now she was out of the hateful Quarter and into more familiar territory. This was one of the oldest residential areas in the city. Once it had been the grandest, but the smart rich kept moving outwards, and now the old villas with their high walls and peeling white paint and overgrown gardens only had a charm for those who liked shabby grandeur.

There was no-one about or so she thought. A flickering street lamp lit up calm broad spaces, carved doorways, ancient undulating roofs. She could see her house in the distance, and noticed that the street gate was open. Somebody had been out with the black paint, leaving graffiti – a barred oval shape that looked faintly familiar.

The boy came out of the shadows silently, and hissed in her ear. 'You Livia?'

She knew him vaguely – a pleb urchin who lived nearby – a cleaner's son perhaps. He had spiky light yellow hair and a spread of freckles. An unwashed smell came off him as he sidled up to Livvy. She thought at first he might be trying to rob her, but then she noticed that he held a note in his hand.

'Here,' he whispered. 'He said I *had* to give it to you personal.'

'Who did?'

'Him. This bloke. Don't know his name. But he said, you had to read it straightaway, before you went home.'

She reached out to take it, but he withdrew his hand.

'Said you'd give me something for it.'

'Cheek,' she said, and was about to walk off.

'Dark-haired bloke. Seen you with him. Blue scarf.'

Max always wore his old blue scarf like a talisman. It might be a scam after all. But she had a few dinars in her pocket, that she'd saved by not taking the tram. 'Here,' she said, fishing them out.

He sniffed as she dropped the coins into his dirty

palm. But when she said, 'That's all I've got. Now give me the note,' he did so, before disappearing into the shadows like a cat.

She took the piece of paper and moved under the flickering spread of the street lamp to read it. It looked as if it had been scrawled hurriedly on an old scrap of torn paper.

But it was Max's writing all right, his spiky black rather childish scrawl, which always reminded her of Max himself, his thin beaky little face, his dark eyes, his stand-up tousled hair.

> I DIDN'T DO IT.
> DON'T BELIEVE ANYTHING THEY TELL YOU.
> AND BE CAREFUL - THEY WANT YOU NEXT.
> DESTROY THIS NOW.
>
> M

She read it and re-read it several times, but still it didn't make sense. But she memorised it – or tried to – and then tore it up into little pieces and dropped it into a gutter, making sure the bits swirled away in the water.

Then she set off towards her house.

As soon as she reached the gate, she saw with dismay that her brother's horse was there, tethered to a branch of the apple tree. It whinnied and pawed the ground; as she gave it a wide berth, she could feel its hot breath. Like its owner, Tony's horse had a temper.

Llew came out of the doorway with a bucket. He grinned sadistically at her. 'He's waiting for you, miss. And not in a good mood neither.'

Livvy sighed. Through the open front door the

lamplight looked yellow and glowing but the house was not welcoming to her. And even less so as she turned into the living room, to find Tony pacing and pawing as impatiently as his horse, while their mother, draped in a crimson stole, reclined with a long-suffering air on the sofa.

'Where have you been?' Tony barked.

'You know where I've been. Mother must have told you. My music lesson of course.'

'Answering back doesn't suit you, Livia. And under the circumstances . . .'

Livvy sighed. Tony's rare visits were always accompanied by these little turbulences. The world never moved calmly and obediently enough to please Tony. So many little things could go wrong in the life of someone who always had to be right. He could never quite forgive Livvy for being her father's favourite, and he could never quite forgive himself for not having measured up to their father's charisma and confidence. Livvy could see all this in him, but it didn't make it any easier to face Tony's continual spluttery disapprovals.

'You should have been home before dark, darling,' said her mother, who, Livvy knew, would not have noticed her lateness if Tony hadn't been there.

Tony was on duty – he wore combat fatigues in the faded blue of the Thirteenth Cornovians, and his red beret was tucked under his arm. The small bronze bull-head glinted on his shoulder – the only non-military decoration soldiers were allowed to wear. Bits of ribbons, standing in for the medals he would have worn for best, testified to his service overseas – Tony was a valiant and much-travelled campaigner. You couldn't doubt his bravery. But it didn't make him a nicer person.

'Showing us up like this! And after what's happened!'

'What has happened?'

To her surprise Tony stopped pacing and sank down into a chair, his head in his hands. When Llew put his head round the door, Tony looked up and snapped, 'Fetch me a drink. A large whisky.'

Livvy waited in silence until the drink arrived. Tony drained it in one gulp and then said quietly, 'You haven't heard, have you?'

'What's the matter?'

'Commander Lucas is dead.'

'What?' Livvy sounded shocked but she wasn't really. Commander Lucas, recently appointed to take charge of the Wroxeter legion. So what? A thin-faced man on a horse.

'They found him yesterday. Murdered. It's been hushed up but it'll be everywhere by now.'

Murdered! Now, that was shocking. She said, 'I'm sorry, Tony.'

He said shortly, 'You'd better be. It was that nasty little friend of yours that did it.'

2

'*Max?* You can't be serious.'

He gave his sharp barking laugh. 'Oh, so you recognise the description then.'

'Yes. No. But I mean . . .'

Mother, alerted too, sat up on her sofa. 'Tony, darling,' she said. 'Too dreadful. What happened?'

'The Commander was seen alive last night. He said he was going back to his flat to catch up on some paperwork. He was due to inspect a new detachment this morning, at ten. But he didn't turn up. His adjutant went to his flat and knocked. When there was no answer, they broke the door down. He was there,' Tony's controlled voice cracked with emotion, 'lying on the floor, covered in blood. He'd been stabbed, Livia, stabbed.'

'But that's awful. Really. So why . . .'

Tony had got hold of himself now. He faced her with steely eyes. 'Because,' he said, answering her question before she had formulated it, 'one of the night security patrol saw your friend Max sidling down the stairs, at about two-thirty in the morning. He recognised him because of his father. He said good evening and your friend "looked startled" apparently.'

'But that's no crime, Tony, being on a stairway at night. Max must still know lots of people in the cohort.'

'In Commander Lucas's room they found a scarf. A long blue scarf. Several people have identified it as belonging to Madoc . . .'

Livvy's mouth fell open. Even Tony's words didn't convince her that Max could have killed Commander Lucas. But she could picture him now, in that scarf, wrapped several times around his chin, his urchin face and dark spiky hair peeking out appealingly.

'Tony, if he'd killed Commander Lucas, he wouldn't be so stupid as to leave his scarf behind!'

'That's for the police to decide,' said Tony briskly.

'I always said he was a strange boy. Didn't I? Didn't I, Tony?' said Livvy's mother. It was nearly time for her next pill and she was growing querulous.

'But what does he say? He must have an alibi.'

'Max Madoc cannot be found,' said Tony. 'He's vanished. And you still want to believe he's innocent.'

'But . . . there must be some explanation.'

'There is. He's guilty. And it compromises all of us.'

'All of us? How?'

'I don't have to spell it out. Everyone knows that our fathers were very close, that he's connected with our family. And also that you and he gad around together without a chaperone in a most undesirable manner.'

'I've tried telling her,' said their mother in an injured voice, 'but she won't listen. She takes after Papa in that.'

'No-one's blaming you, Mother,' said Tony in irritation. 'Livia should know better herself. Well, it's not too late. Something's about to happen that will push Miss Livia back into respectability.'

'What do you mean?' Livvy said in alarm.

'You'll find out soon enough. Llew, fetch my jacket, will you.'

'You won't stay for supper, darling?'

Tony went over and gave his mother a perfunctory kiss on the head. 'Not now, dear. I have to be back in barracks soon.' Livvy he did not kiss.

As he reached the door, they heard the siren of the curfew echoing eerily in the already empty streets. He gave Livvy a look. 'Soon you'll learn to respect things like order,' he said.

As an army officer, he was not subject to curfew. Livvy watched him striding out into the yard, shouting impatiently at Llew. Fear for Max and anxiety for herself began to tighten in her throat.

Back in the house, Minna came in with a tablet and a glass of water on a tray. Already her mother seemed to be forgetting Tony's visit. 'How nice,' she said in a little cosy mouse-like voice, as she reached for the tablet. 'What about playing me something on your violin, Livvy, before we have dinner?'

Livvy found out soon enough what Tony had meant. The following morning at eight o'clock there was a heavy knock on the outside door. Livvy had just got dressed, and since the servants were busy with the breakfast, she opened it herself.

Two big men in army uniform stood there. They wore the blue uniform of Tony's legion. 'Morning, Miss Livia,' said one of them amiably. 'Get your bag packed. This could be your lucky day.'

They were so big that she fell back before them like water. Soon they were in the vestibule, seeming to fill it up. 'Nice plants,' said one, looking around at the trough of myrtle and orange bushes that Minna looked after so carefully.

Livvy's mother appeared on the stairway, still in her floating morning robe. Her unmade-up face was pink and bemused, haloed by her soft hair. She had been a great beauty in her youth, and you could still see it, even when she was bleary and dishevelled.

'Livvy?' she said. 'What's the matter?'

'Please don't trouble yourself, madam,' said one of the two men. 'Privates Owen and Moroni at your service. We've come to take Miss Livia away with us.'

'*What?*' said Livvy.

'Your place at the college has just come up, miss. Congratulations.'

'What place? What college?'

'Why, at Ishtar College of course. Where else?'

14

'But I don't understand. I wasn't down for a place at Ishtar.'

'Didn't you know about it? Well then, miss, what a nice surprise.'

'Mother, did you know about this?'

'What, dear?'

'They say I've got a place at Ishtar.'

'Have you, dear? How nice.'

'Did you put my name down without telling me?'

'Me? I don't recall. Maybe.'

'Then it must have been Tony. Mother, I can't go!'

'Why not? It has a very good reputation.'

'But, Mother! You know how Father felt about the Order.'

'And much good that did him, miss, if you don't mind my saying,' put in one of the soldiers. Livvy ignored him.

Her father had always been against the power of religion – any of the religions – and he especially disliked the secretiveness of the Mithraic Order. But he had not denied its antiquity. On the other hand, he claimed that the cult of Ishtar as it existed now was little more than a hundred years old, and had simply been thought up as a way of quietening the wives and daughters of men who belonged to the Order.

'Well, if we're to get there this morning, you'd better go and pack, miss. Now,' said one of the soldiers, and his voice though still friendly had a steely note to it.

As though she was seeing it for the last time, Livvy stared round her at the vestibule of her house – the sweeping stairway, the scabbed pink paintwork, the dingy gilt mirrors, the oil-paintings of long forgotten great-grandparents. She saw it as the soldiers must be

15

seeing it, a shabby house belonging to a family who had once been grand and were no longer important. How those men must be despising her mother, who now fluttered downstairs and with the graciousness that she could still muster, invited them to sit down, to take a drink.

Livvy did not know what she was supposed to pack, or what would happen to anything that she might leave behind. In the end, she took very little, a few changes of clothing, her hairbrush and toothbrush, a couple of favourite books, a photograph of her father and a china model of a dog which had always sat on her desk. She did not take her jewellery such as it was, her dear old stuffed elephant or her violin – she had no intention of making a permanent settlement in Ishtar.

Before too long, she was on the road, seated in the back of an old army carriage, rattling along. Outside, people were going to work or opening up shops and workplaces. There was a smell of fresh wood smoke on the air and the greasy tang of a hundred breakfasts. She had not yet had her own, but she felt sick rather than hungry.

They went through the wide suburban streets – past quiet houses impassive behind their walls, past the rows of little red-brick boxes where the respectable citizens lived and tended their tiny patches of vegetables, past the bleak barracks where a detachment of Military Police had their quarters, past the smoky mazes of the industrial zone and out into the countryside. Women hustled trails of lowing cows, heavy with milk, towards milking sheds, men mended wheels in their yards and children teased the family chickens. The great hills, faded green and deep gold and russet in the declining

16

year, grew closer and filled the window-space. Everything was wilder beyond those hills to the west – somewhere in their depths were the Wolves – the *Bleiddiaid* – who were supposed to have started the riots ten years ago. Sometimes you saw their dagger-sign scrawled on walls or gouged on stones left by the road. They were part of the Cymric language revival in Britain and planned to overthrow the Empire – as though, her teacher had said scornfully, a gnat could overthrow a lion!

But Max had been drawn to them recently, she knew that. He scribbled daggers on walls and then rubbed them out hastily with his arm; he hummed Cymric songs under his breath; words like 'repression' and 'liberation' had found their way into his vocabulary. Of course she shared some of his views: votes for everyone – including, especially, women. And – unlike Tony – she was proud of her own Cymric connections. But she didn't trust Max's common sense to keep him out of trouble.

There had always been something a little dangerous and unpredictable about Max – as a child he would take breathtaking risks, climbing rocky walls or swinging over rivers on frail ropes. She was scared for him. He could be heading for all sorts of difficulties. But he was not a killer.

And he would certainly not want to kill Commander Lucas who'd been good to Max and his family after their father's death.

Both their fathers dead – his through suicide, hers through a silly accident – it was as though they belonged to the same troubled family. And though he'd grown apart from her over the last few years, she'd seen enough of him to know that he was still basically the same Max, with the same daft sense of humour.

The carriage turned off now down a deep woody lane. Sometimes she caught glimpses of the golden stone of rich villas through the trees. Farm children playing in their yards ran cheekily after the soldiers; sheepdogs tried to round up the carriage.

And then they came to a pair of old gates, set deep in the trees. The lichened stone was crested with a long-obsolete family shield – but above it a new sign in gleaming brass said ISHTAR COLLEGE.

The carriage turned through the gates. A thick band of trees separated the young ladies from the gaze of the world, but beyond it, the drive curved out into a sweep of exquisitely manicured gardens, shrubs, Italian conifers, bushes still scented even in November.

And beyond, the long, low, colonnaded expanse of the restored villa. She'd heard it said that no expense had been spared setting up Ishtar – and it was easy to believe. Girls walked laughing and confident across the lawns, dressed in white tunics, swinging rackets, or carrying riding helmets. It was all so different from Sixth Precinct Girls, the school to which she should have returned that morning.

Finally, the carriage jolted to a halt, and as one of the men jumped down to let her out with a mocking bow, the great bronze-embossed doors of the college swung slowly open.

It was as though they were waiting for her.

# 3

A small maidservant dressed in sparrow brown curtsied deeply before Livvy. 'Wait here, please while I tell Mother Superior.'

Livvy waited in a long vestibule. New pink marble reflected from the walls like mirrors, ornate gilded moulding fretted the ceiling and little gold-and-rose chairs perched on the shining wooden floor. A sickly statue of Mother Ishtar, crowned with stars in a long blue dress, held out a hand to an eager schoolgirl. Invisible central heating kept the air dry and oppressively warm; and a huge bunch of orange hothouse lilies added their heady perfume. So unlike the scruffy upstairs room of Sixth Precinct Girls, with its malodorous oil stove and peeling paintwork!

Soon a woman came gliding across the parquet floor to meet her. She was small and plump-breasted, dressed in a long gown of pigeon-grey. She wore no jewellery except the small silver brooch of a star and a scrap of purple ribbon that Livvy recognised as one of the Levels of the Ishtarian Order. Her soft greying hair was teased into a low chignon; her eyes were large and grey. She greeted Livvy with an outstretched hand and a smile that had just the merest splinter of ice in it.

'You must be Livia,' she said. 'We're very pleased to have you here. We all admired your father so much.'

Livvy decided to start as she meant to go on. 'I didn't want to come here. I was made to.'

Once again the ice glittered in the smile. 'We have a saying here that Desire and Destiny don't work together. You'll be glad you came, one day.'

And then, because Livvy did not respond, she went

19

on, 'Places in College are like gold-dust. But you have friends in very high places. Think yourself lucky, my dear. Now. I am your Mother Superior. You will call me Mother. You will start, as everyone starts, at White Level, and then, when you have been here a little while, and learned some things, you will progress to Emerald. How far you go after that depends on you. But you'll find that the benefits, both material and spiritual, are well worth the climb. Mmm?'

She must have taken Livvy's silence for assent, for she said, 'Come this way, now. I'll find someone to show you around.'

She found Amanda, a small dark-eyed girl with a tinkly little laugh, who wore a calf-length dress of Ishtar blue with a dark red sash pinned by a silver star over one shoulder. Amanda, summoned from her common room, wiped the traces of laughter from her face and dropped a deep curtsey to Mother Superior – curtseying was a skill Livvy was clearly going to have to acquire.

'Amanda, I want you to meet Livia Marcel. She's just come to join us today. I'd like you to show her around, tell her what to expect. Mmm?'

Then she turned and left them, tip-tipping away down the corridor. Amanda flashed a complicit grin at Livvy. 'She *nearly* caught us playing a wicked game of cards!' she confided. 'Oh, we would have been in trouble! Ask me any questions, only I don't promise answers! Now where shall we start? Well, here's Crimson Common Room. You'll be in White, of course.'

She opened the door, and Livvy saw a sea of faces. 'This is Livvy, everyone.'

A chorus of 'Hi, Livvy!' Everyone smiled. All wore long blue dresses and crimson sashes. Livvy's head swam.

Amanda took her around. Here was the White Common Room, where she would meet her companions. More smiling faces – blue dresses, white sashes. 'Hi, Livvy!' As though they'd known her for ever.

They climbed sweeping stairs. At the top was another shining corridor, another little shrine to Mother Ishtar. The Emerald Common Room, the Chestnut, the Gold, the Lilac, the Turquoise, the Violet.

Half a dozen girls burst out of Violet, laughing and hugging each other in the highest excitement. They wore purple sashes. She heard: 'Oh, my *dear!* . . . Ooh ooh! . . . How exciting! . . . Oh, *well* done, you!'

'What are they so excited about?'

'Well, Julia – that's the tall girl in the middle – she's just got engaged.'

'Engaged? I thought you weren't supposed to have anything to do with boys here.'

Amanda giggled and put her hands over her mouth. 'No, worst luck! The fuss if we did! But they've found her the most gorgeous man. He's second-in-command of his legion; he's forty years old; he's a widower with a little girl; and apparently he's an absolute dish! We're all so jealous. But it'll be our turn soon, just you wait and see!'

'You mean, they arrange marriages for you?'

'Well, of course. How else are we supposed to get married?'

'But that's dreadful!'

'No, it's not. We'd never meet men half so gorgeous without College. Ishtar girls are the best; everybody wants them. I'm really looking forward to when it's my turn.'

'I'd rather be left to choose for myself, thank you.'

'Oh?' said Amanda. 'Livvy, do you know what the divorce rate is for ordinary marriages? *We* hardly ever get divorced. Anyway, let's not fight about this now. There's still so much to see. Now what sports do you do? I'll show you the gym.'

She was not to be left alone. Usually it was Amanda who shadowed her like a soft little mother hen, but if not Amanda, then one of the others. Mona, Portia, Nerys, bright and giggly, shared her dorm, along with eager-to-please and horribly grateful Lila. There was always a friendly arm to be slipped through hers or a head poked round the door with 'Come on, Livia, don't sit moping on your own. Come and join us for . . .' And there would be a game, or a gossip or an activity that needed her presence. She found too on that first day, that her own clothes had been whisked away never to reappear and in their place was laid out the heavy blue woollen dress of the winter uniform, complete with white sash.

Livvy remembered how her father had always spoken of the Orders and the stranglehold they were getting over the army. 'Secretive codswallop,' he said, 'most of it is. But it's also dangerous codswallop. Never trust a man who offers you simple answers to complicated questions, Liv – you can bet your life he's hiding something from you.'

What was being hidden from them here? Every morning at nine-thirty they sat down for lessons – and how different were the light comfortable classrooms with their blonde wood furniture, glossy textbooks and odourless central heating from the scabby upstairs room of Sixth Precinct.

Another difference of course was that in her old school, they learned things. This was partly because of

22

their teacher, Donald Macdonald, an old Scot with a drink problem who'd been kicked out of a smart boys' school in the south. But he was deemed good enough to teach girls.

Which he did, and marvellously, most of the time. When he was too slurred, or too hung-over to teach, the girls closed ranks, made him cups of black coffee and entertained themselves, reading or testing each other on last week's lessons. They knew that girls didn't usually get the chances they were getting – history, science, Classical Latin and Greek. Don, when sober, brought everything to life before them. When he taught Homer, they could hear the clash of sword on sun-heated armour, smell the wine-dark sea and the thyme in the air, watch Cassandra running wildly over the battlements, or Achilles striding sulkily over the dawn-grey beach. He loved Ancient History especially, and spent hours describing the centurions of the old days with their glittering breastplates and plumed helmets, the marble splendours of Old Rome, the purple togas and laurel crowns, the gilded *fasces*, the monuments, the temples and columns, the gardens cascading down the hills.

'New Rome may be a beautiful place, I dinna doubt that, but to my way of thinking, not a patch on Old Rome. Even though it's just for the tourists, you must go there, girls. Drink in the history. And to think it nearly fell to the vandals. Imagine that, girls. Imagine what the world would be like now if Rome had fallen – and it might well have done. Think what a world we'd be living in now. Thank the gods – if you believe in them, which I'm glad to say I don't – that Rome, held out, and is still here, a thousand and some years later.' That was Don; scornful of all modern movements; he wanted to see a restoration of Rome to some ideal Golden Age, a Golden Age to be reached by reading enough Old Latin poetry . . .

'I'll drink to that, Don!' one of the others – Helen, was it, or Portia? – had called out naughtily. And Don, whose voice was starting to show its end of afternoon bleariness – he kept a hip-flask hidden behind *Caesar's Gallic Wars* – pretended to be angry at her. 'Wicked wee girl! If you were a lad, I'd have beaten you for cheek!'

Livvy felt herself smiling as she remembered Don, but all there was now was the genteel drone of Sister Prudentia of the Order, reading an unconscionably dreary Ishtarian girls' classic novel, *Elena's Sacrifice*, to a class dutifully and silently stitching away. She wondered whether anyone had bothered to tell Don, and her old friends, Helen, Portia and the rest, why she hadn't come back that morning. Her mother certainly wouldn't have done so. Had anyone come knocking at her front gate? What were they being told?

She had been at Ishtar a week, and already it was hard to remember the outside world. So perfectly, so softly, Ishtar and its ways closed around you and over your head, like a softly scented sea. Nothing was harsh or unpleasant. The food was good; the beds were soft; the hours of lessons were short. As well as sewing, she was to learn water-colour painting, singing, a little poetry and a whole mound of Ishtarian doctrine. Playing the violin was approved of, so even though she had left hers behind, another instrument was found for her, a beautiful one, far finer than her own, and a place in the school orchestra promised. 'Gosh, you are lucky, Livvy! Girls'd *kill* to be in the orchestra! They're going on a European tour next year!'

24

The main purpose of the schedule was to take pupils through the Ishtarian Levels. In about a month, they promised her, she'd be able to take the test for Emerald. There'd be a ceremony with secret rites. 'And then you'll *really* be one of us!' If she passed through the succeeding Levels – a process which usually took three years – she'd be found a nice army husband. Then she'd be taken away, to live in an army apartment in one of the cities, or a secluded villa in the country, to manage her servants and bear lots of children.

Her husband, of course, would belong to the Order of Mithras, and he wouldn't be expected to race through his Levels of Initiation as quickly as the girls were pushed through theirs. For men, it might be a lifetime's journey to work through to the upper Levels. But you'd be part of a secret fellowship that would help you in all the aspects of your life. Materially, at least, as an Ishtar graduate, married to a Mithraist, you'd have a good and secure life.

But Livvy could not forget her father saying, 'I'll look after my own life, thanks very much. I don't need those creeps to arrange things for me.' And it wasn't until after his death that Tony had joined the movement – she wondered now whether they'd targeted him like she was being sucked in now.

Only she didn't think, however relentless the propaganda, however warm and safe the atmosphere, however fine the prospects, she was really going to be happy here, or pushed into an arranged marriage. Did anyone drop out of Ishtar? No-one would give Livvy a straight answer. 'We don't like to talk about things like that,' was all anyone would say. And 'Oh, Livvy, dear, must you think of such horrible things?'

And, although the regime wasn't a taxing one, every moment of the day was structured one way or another. All sorts of little competitions and ceremonies kept the girls' interest afloat – there was a monthly prize for the prettiest common room (displays of flowers and watercolours and hand-sewn cushions), the concert for Mother Superior's birthday, the end-of-year awards to individual girls (Greatest Improvement over the Year; Disability most Bravely Overcome; Cheerfulness; Best Dancer; Best Cook, and so on). There were little parties to be held to celebrate a girl's engagement, or her leaving, or the triumphs of alumni. 'Guess what, Monica Markus has just had *twins!*' And then of course the succession of secret rites which marked rising through the Levels. Livvy could expect little time to herself here. She was allowed to write a letter once a week but only to members of her family. The first time she wrote, a brief and languid reply came from her mother. 'I do miss you of course, darling, but I know you'll be having a wonderful time.' And there was a pompous burst from Tony. 'It is a matter of great pride to our family that you are now . . .' etc etc. One communication from each, and then no more, even though she sent off her permitted letter every week.

Well, give her half a chance, and Tony could stuff his great family pride. But how was she ever going to get out of here, and where would she go if she did get out?

# 4

Not for the first time, Livvy noticed the little sparrow-brown maidservant who'd opened the door to her on her arrival.

Usually the servants kept themselves to themselves. You hardly saw them, except sometimes scuttling into a dorm with a clean pile of linen, or whisking away plates from the refectory. To Livvy's fellow pupils, servants were just an invisible part of the mechanics that kept life running smoothly; it wouldn't occur to them to notice the servants, still less talk to them. But from time to time, she caught this girl looking at her, in a pensive, guarded manner. Her name, Livvy knew, was Bronwen, and she spoke with a strong Cymric accent. But that was all Livvy knew about her.

The weeks had passed. Initiation time was drawing near for Emerald, and the girls were being whipped up into an almost hysterical state of excitement. Eight others were scheduled to go through the ceremony with Livvy, including poor sad Lila, plain, clumsy and overweight, who'd not been smart enough to go through it on the previous two occasions. The truth was, though Lila was too slow and trusting to see it, that the poor girl was never going to be decorative enough to be an army wife, nor smart enough to join the unmarried Ishtarian Sisters who ran the colleges. Lila studied hard, and was always roping the others in to test her. 'Please Livvy, just hear me on the Ten Points! I'm sure I've got them now!'

Livvy wondered whether she too could avoid being pushed through the Levels by pretending to be stupid. But the demands for passing Emerald were so simple that it was almost harder to fail than to pass.

So the ceremony was set for three days' time. Emerald Level Ishtarians were true Ishtarians, not mere novices. The more she was sucked into the system, the harder it would be to ever get out of it.

It was a cold December morning and the grass was glazed with frost. Red berries glowed in the bare hedges. Livvy had been playing a game of rackets with three other girls. They had just left the gymnasium, a modern, purpose-built block just across the lawn from the main building, when Livvy realised she'd left her sports bag behind. She told the others to go on – it was too cold to hang about waiting for her – and dashed back into the building, realising as she did so, that this was almost the only time she'd been left alone. So she took as long as possible to find her bag.

The little maid was in the building too – piling plates onto a tray.

Livvy left the gym and set off slowly across the icy grass. She was cold, in her long dress and light wrap – Ishtarian girls weren't really expected to spend time outside in the cold, ruining their complexions. The little servant girl came past her with the tray, walking rather fast, and overtook her.

Then when they were both just halfway across the expanse of lawn, the girl tripped. She fell over, tray and contents scattering everywhere.

Livvy ran to help. Already she could see the grey figure of Sister Prudentia, the Novice Mistress, standing at the side door of the college waiting for her. But she couldn't leave the poor girl grovelling in the frosty grass.

She knelt down next to the girl. A plate and a glass had been broken, cutlery and bowls lay around. 'Let me help you.'

But the little brown girl hissed, in a low voice, 'Don't look surprised. When I tell you something, don't look surprised.'

'What?' said Livvy, feeling herself doing just that.

'Get your head down. Listen to me; only don't show it.'

Livvy had got the point now. She reached over to grab a plate. The girl, also bending down, said softly, 'You can't talk in College. Anywhere. There are listening devices. I'll only say this once. I've got a message from your friend.'

'My friend?'

'You know who I mean. Him. Dark, short hair.'

'Max?' breathed Livvy.

'He's not Max now. He's one of us. Gwydion. Take this.' And while she seemed to be reaching out for a fallen knife, she manoeuvred out of her sleeve a roll of paper that had been tucked away there.

'Read it in the toilets with the door shut, tear it up and flush it away, right? And remember you're in danger. All the time you're in danger. Oh dear, this broken glass. Thank you ever so much, miss.'

And Livvy looked up to see Sister Prudentia gliding across the frozen grass towards them.

'Very clumsy of you, Bronwen,' she said. 'Those breakages will be deducted from your wages. Livia, a word, please.'

Livvy scrambled to her feet, tucking the roll of paper into her own sleeve as she did so.

'Young ladies are not expected to help the servants,' said the sister. 'Servants take the consequence for their own carelessness. Now please hurry back to class. There's a rehearsal in fifteen minutes.'

It wasn't until after the rehearsal that Livvy managed to get to the toilets on her own, in a way that didn't look suspicious. She locked the door, and pulled the paper from her sleeve.

In fact there were two bits of paper rolled tightly together.

She unrolled them and peered to read in the dingy light. But Max's familiar handwriting jumped out at her.

THEY ARE ON TO YOU TOO. THIS IS A COPY
OF YOUR SECRET POLICE DOSSIER.
YOU MUST GET AWAY.
GET TO THE BLACK DRAGON BY THE DOCKS.
AS SOON AS YOU CAN!!!!!!!!!!!
M. (GWYDION )

The other piece of paper was a rough photocopy on brittle shiny paper. It was so marked and blotchy that she could scarcely read the uneven type.

At the top was her name.

### LIVIA MARCEL

Daughter of Felix Marcel – deceased. Mother (Antonia Marcel née Rheged) has been confirmed in a drug habit. Brother – Anthony Marcel – is a member of the Order (Beta Level). His 'loyalty' to the Order is beyond suspicion though he must be prevented from reaching the Brotherhood. Suitable posting abroad recommended.

Marcel is an associate of Max Madoc. This and her level of awareness and insubordination renders her dangerous. Also the latest intelligence from GF suggests more than this. Arrangements are being made at present to expedite her admission to I. Coll. However it is felt that this may not be sufficient to neutralise her. (Plans for Madoc have already been implemented.)

Elimination therefore under active consideration. Keep under constant surveillance.

Livvy stared at the words as though the force of her eyes could make them disappear, or change into something harmless.

She didn't know how long she'd been standing there in the gloom when she heard a knocking on the door. 'Livvy! Are you in there?' called someone – Amanda, or Juliana or Phoebe. 'You've been ages!'

'Just coming!' she called, hearing her own voice cracking like a stranger's. 'Bad period pains. Won't be long.'

And with one more look at the letter to burn it into her skull (*drug habit . . . dangerous . . . elimination),* she tore both the dossier and Max's note into tiny pieces and flushed them away.

That night, she lay awake for hours in the darkness, listening to the gentle breathing of the girls in her dorm. She tried to remember every word that she had read, sometimes doubting her memory – if only she'd kept the dossier just a little longer before destroying it.

She could hardly believe what it seemed to suggest. Had her mother's drug habit been – somehow – engineered? Livvy tried to remember back to the time before her father died. Three years ago now. But then she had been a child, and not old enough to question adult behaviour. She never expected her mother to be

31

warm and affectionate the way her father was. It was always her father, busy though he was, who told her stories and made time for little expeditions, while her mother had her hair done, or shopped for clothes. There were the little pills – to steady her nerves, Mother said. Livvy never questioned that her mother's nerves were something special that needed to be steadied.

But back then she could never remember her mother looking dishevelled or sounding slurred. That came later.

After Father had died, everyone had been so good to them. Including lovely Dr Claude, the army doctor, whom they'd known for so many years. Always glad to visit night or day, always running up little prescriptions . . .

Could it be? *Could* it?

And there was something nagging away at her – a feeling that her father somehow *knew* things that were dangerous to know. As did Max's father.

And because of what they'd known . . .

No. It was too horrible to think of.

But there was one word in the dossier that wasn't speculation. It seemed to jump out at her in huge screaming letters.

*Elimination.*

The next morning, when she awoke, there was already a buzz and hubbub. 'Have you heard?' said the girls. 'Dreadful! I saw her only yesterday! Awful!'

At first, with her own problems to think about – she had lain awake most of the night and only dozed off just after dawn – she couldn't really summon up much interest in whatever was arousing their concern.

But when she had dressed and gone out into the corridor, she found out what it was that had happened, early that morning, so early that nobody, except perhaps some of the kitchen servants, had been around. Certainly no-one had witnessed anything.

'Didn't you know?' said a girl at Chestnut Level, her hair still in its nocturnal plaits. 'It was that nice little maid. What was her name? Blodwen? Bronwen? Yes, that's right. Must have fallen downstairs. Neck broken. *Awful.* Poor thing!'

# 5

Livvy had always imagined that she wanted excitement out of life. Not the sort of wild excitement that Max, with his dangerous streak, had craved, of course, but just *something,* to add a little variety and spice to the calm domestic life of a Roman-British girl. Just something to be a little different from the crowd.

And now here she was, with as much excitement as anyone could want. And she didn't like it, one bit. She wanted it to go away, not to be happening. She wanted to get on with her life.

And until yesterday she could have done just that.

It was nearing the end of term at Ishtar College. Though end of term did not necessarily mean vacations. *We like our girls to be* really *settled before they go back out into the world again.*

But it did mean that just for a while, the usually rigid routines were breaking up just a little. For most of the initiation ceremonies would be held now, the Solstice being one of the auspicious times of the year. In addition, Mother Superior had her birthday in two weeks' time, and a special concert was being arranged for her. Girls divided themselves up into a number of groups – this time not related to their Levels – and arranged little concerts, playlets, recitals, according to their skills. These would be rehearsed and rehearsed and then performed, no expense spared in terms of costume and settings.

Livvy had already found herself solicited by several groups. Some wanted her to play the violin; others wanted her to act. She had put off the decision so far. But now she just might be able to turn her indecision to her advantage.

That morning was one of the most difficult of her life. With everything in her head screaming out, she had to force herself to sit still and pretend to listen to a dreary sermon about the love of Mother Ishtar. One thing was clear above everything else – she had to get out of Ishtar!

But how? And where would she go?

Not home, certainly. The system which had managed to get her sent here would certainly be watching out for her at home. Might even involve Tony in getting her sent back to Ishtar as soon as possible. Poor Tony. It looked as though he too, with his deep loyalty to Mithras, was no more than a dupe in all of this.

Then there was the place Max had mentioned in his note: the Black Dragon, near the docks. That reference more than anything else convinced her that the note really was from Max, and he was on her side. The dock area had always been their secret place. Max would know that she could find her way about. The Black Dragon. Wherever it was, she'd find it . . .

So that was one thing. The other problem was more urgent. Just how did she get out of here? Listening devices everywhere, Bronwen had said. Poor Bronwen. Somebody had been listening to *her*, all right.

Somebody here was her enemy. Everyone was watching her, of course, but somebody was watching her in a special way.

So she had to get out. Get out now.

Which was easily said. But not so easy to do. Gradually, as Sister's voice droned on and on, she began to assemble the bits of her escape plan, as though she was putting together a jigsaw.

By midday she had the plan more or less worked out. But whether the escape would work as well as the plan, was yet to be seen.

Time seemed to stand still as the day advanced. Livvy was conscious of every minute passing, felt the dragging pulse of the hours with her own heartbeat. After the Ishtar sermon came an embroidery lesson – and never had her fingers seemed so clumsy. 'Are you all right, Livvy?' asked Hermione, one of her Emerald Level 'friends'. 'You look ever so pale.'

'Bad period pains,' said Livvy.

'Poor dear! Go to the Infirmary. Sister's *marvellous*.'

She ate nothing for lunch. Girls sympathised with her. Some gave her things to take, herbal pills or 'simply marvellous' compounds. There was no way Livvy would let anyone slip her something strange, so she smiled a weak period-pain smile and pretended to put things away for later.

Then there was an afternoon of lessons. An art-appreciation class and some current affairs – after all, a legionary's wife must know what was going on in the world. Livia listened to a simplistic account of the wars in Greece. Tony had served in Thrace so she knew all about them. He'd won his medals there too, for bravery. Quite deserved, probably. For all his faults, Tony was no coward. In fact no-one had expected him to return from that mission . . . Livia suddenly sat up, as she remembered it. Had someone been trying to *eliminate* Tony too?

And what reason would anyone have to suspect her family? Why should her association with Max render her dangerous? Now she remembered something one of her father's old sergeants had said to her, when he'd met her in the street outside the barracks. 'If I were you, miss, I'd ask young Madoc to mind his mouth a bit. There are things he's been saying that aren't going to do you or your family any good, if you get my meaning. He's too fond of sitting in the Spread Eagle and sharing his ideas with all and sundry. Get him to shut up, I would.' At the time, she'd not taken much notice. She knew Max was wild, and not everyone liked it. But just supposing his ideas weren't so wild, and too close to the truth?

But still, she and her family had nothing to do with that. What was happening?

Late afternoon, and the maid came round to light the lamps. The nervous knot in Livvy's stomach tightened. This was worse than any period pain.

The lesson over, girls began to chat about which group they were going to choose for Mother Superior's birthday. *Well, I think I'll go for choral singing. I'm going to be wicked and go for the musical. I've always wanted to act. Wonder if I dare?* And then the repeated chorus: *What about you, Livvy?*

Livvy tried, with a voice that had no breath in it, to sound relaxed. 'Well, I haven't quite made up my mind. I *ought* to go for the violin group, but I quite fancy the play too. Or maybe the singing would be fun.' The important thing to convey was that *she hadn't made up her mind.*

And then, at the end of the afternoon, there was a brief period of chaos, as girls milled about, going to the rooms of their choice. This was the only time of the day when she could put her plan into action. It wouldn't last long, and if she missed it, she might be too late. Even now, that unknown person might be watching her.

So, for a while, she swilled round with the groups of girls. Only she didn't go into any of the rooms. Instead, she went up the stairs to the dorm.

The corridor was in darkness now, a deep granular darkness that seemed to absorb sounds as well. So when Sister Prudentia suddenly loomed at her out of the shadows, she gasped. 'Oh, Sister!' Livvy exclaimed, trying to sound girlish. 'You did give me a fright!'

'Why aren't you on your way to the rehearsals, Livia?' said Sister, in her cool, expressionless voice.

Luckily, the right excuse came plausibly to hand. 'Oh I am, Sister. Only I've left my violin in the dorm; I'm just off to fetch it now.'

'Mind you aren't late,' was all Sister said, and she glided away into the shadows.

The first thing was to find something to wear. A girl seen out in blue Isthar-robes would be conspicuous and her own clothes had been taken away.

However, there were blankets on their beds, large fine woollen blankets of grey with a soft stripe in them. In appearance they were not unlike the shawls worn by women from the mountain lands. She could cover herself with a blanket, thus hiding at least some of her blue dress. That was one thing.

The next was how to escape. The front door was out of the question of course. And she didn't know the servants' quarters well enough to sneak out through there.

There were two other side exits that she was aware of. One was on the ground floor. This led almost directly into a shrubbery where she could hide successfully. But to get to it she would have to pass directly in front of the Staff Room. Sisters were always coming in and out. She couldn't risk that.

The other exit was, on the face of it, much better. It was on the first floor, in a quiet corridor not far from her dorm. It was a fire door, though the girls often used it when they were in a hurry. A flight of steps led down to a windowless wall. But it meant crossing a huge expanse of lawn to get to safety. Anyone watching would have a clear view of her. She would have to rely on the fast falling darkness to protect her.

Once she had crossed the lawn, there was the shelter of a band of trees. And the big stone wall around the college, although beautifully kept around the entrance, was crumbling in some places. Near a derelict farmhouse just beyond the gym block, several gaps led directly through into the countryside.

In the dorm, she stripped the blanket from her bed – folding back the white cotton coverlet so it didn't look disturbed – and rolled it up as small as possible. She scanned her few possessions ranged on the bedside table. Nothing of any use. She didn't have any money or even anything she could sell.

Ironically, she was starting to feel ravenously hungry. Of course she'd been able to eat very little since she'd got the message from Bronwen, and it occurred to her that she ought to have taken some fruit or a piece of bread with her. Well, too late now.

Silently, she crept through the dorm and out into the corridor. She had a short walk, which would lead her past the main staircase again, and then a sharp turn to the fire-escape door. She was conscious of each footfall.

Then suddenly, a splash of light and an explosion of noise burst out before her.

A group of four girls, carrying a lamp, ran up the stairs, laughing and shouting. Livvy tried to shrink back against the wall, but it was too late.

'Livvy, Livvy!'

'Sly puss! Where have you been hiding?'

'We *need* you, Liv, in our play!'

'You *promised!*'

Livvy stood with her back to the wall, the blanket tucked behind her.

'Oh, hi,' she said weakly. 'I wasn't feeling too well, actually. I was going to lie down for a bit.'

'No, you weren't, you wicked thing,' said one of the girls. 'You're going in the wrong direction.'

'I bet you were sneaking off to Marcia's group.'

'Oh, Liv, you traitor.'

'Well, actually . . .' said Livvy.

'Well, Marcia isn't going to get you! We are! Come on girls, this is a kidnap!' And the four girls grabbed Livvy by the arm, giggling and shrieking, and started to frog-march her down the stairs.

Livvy let her blanket fall to the floor. Luckily no-one noticed it, or they might have asked why she was carrying a blanket around with her. 'I'll come quietly,' she said, trying to sound light-hearted.

Together the group marched down the stairs, and

towards the room where they were holding their rehearsal.

The door opened and Livvy was pushed inside triumphantly.

The group was enacting a classic one-act playlet called *The Fashionable Tea*. Written two hundred years ago, it satirised a woman who'd suddenly come into money and her attempt to win over the local aristocratic ladies of her district by holding a tea-party. Dated and innocuous, it was much loved by girls' schools and amateur dramatic groups. Livvy had seen it several times already.

Someone thrust a script into her hands. 'Come along now, Livvy, it's all decided. You're going to be the maid.'

The maid was chirpy and irrepressible, and her comic ripostes were meant to make a commentary on her mistress's pretensions. More hands pushed Livvy to the centre of the room, where furniture had been moved to make an acting space.

'Right,' said the girl in charge, a big girl at Crimson Level, called Sylvia, 'now *everyone's* deigned to turn up,' – with a sarcastic glance at Livvy – 'we can get going. We'll start off with Petronilla's entrance in Act Two. Cora, you start off with *Oh, I always . . .*'

Cora was a very bad actress, Livvy noticed. 'Oh, I always purchase my clothes from the Continent,' she declaimed.

Someone pushed Livvy from behind. Today she was acting badly too. 'Oh, madam,' she said, 'who could guess that shawl came from the flea market?' Well, two hundred years ago, they might have laughed.

The rehearsal creaked on. By now it was dark

outside. A smell of soup wafted in from the kitchens. Soon the rehearsal would break for supper and then the girls would go back to their common room to read, play games and gossip until bedtime.

And then suddenly, chance came to Livvy's rescue.

Cora sat down at a little table and pretended to cut some fruit. She was using a penknife as a prop and suddenly it slipped and sliced into her finger. She screamed, and blood at once began to well from the cut. Everyone rushed around in confusion.

Livvy seized her opportunity. 'I'll go and fetch . . .' she exclaimed and rushed from the room.

She climbed the stairs two at a time. At the top her blanket lay on the floor just where she had dropped it. A minute later she was at the fire door, shoving it open.

Then the icy night air rushed at her and glittering starry darkness surrounded her.


# 6


Her first instinct was to run – down the stairs and across the grass. But the icy grass was treacherous; she slid, and then fell right over, feeling her ankle going beneath her.

'Calm down now, Livia,' she told herself. 'You'll never get anywhere like this.'

Her dress was soaked and her hands hurt where she had flung them out to stop herself falling.

She looked back at windows lit up behind blinds, comforting, secure, glowing. So easy to go back, and slip into the routines again.

Just that one word stopped her – *elimination*!

The ground was soft and uneven and brambles snagged her skirt. Her ankle was starting to hurt and the cold was numbing.

But she didn't let herself stop. Blundering through bushes, trees, potholes, she searched for the wall.

And found it at last, a roughness beneath her hands.

Following it by touch, she did not have to go very far before she found what she was seeking: a pile of tumbled stones. She scrambled through the gap, feeling her dress rip, and at last she was outside the walls.

'And now, Livia Marcel,' she said to herself, 'your troubles are really beginning.'

Perhaps no more than ten minutes had passed since she had rushed from the rehearsal room. Maybe another ten before people realised she was no longer there. The chances were that they would simply wait for her to come back. But if she had not returned by suppertime, then they would start looking. At first, in the house. That would take half an hour or so.

Then what? Would they go out into the night, sisters and College girls to look for her? There were no men present, apart from an ancient caretaker who mended the boilers and an equally ancient gardener. There were no dogs, as far as she knew. Ishtar College really wasn't geared to catch escaping pupils.

But before too long, a search party would set out. And even if the college itself wasn't too anxious to find her, somebody was.

Livia was a city girl through and through. She had spent little time in the countryside, though once she had stayed with her aunt, who had a villa deep in a tree-covered valley further north. The countryside was all right in its place, but it was full of things she did not like, noises, smells, all the unpredictability of Nature. As if to remind her of this, an owl hooted eerily, far too close to her.

She began to shiver with the cold, and remembered the blanket still held beneath her arm. With it flung over her head, the loose end tossed over a shoulder, she wasn't quite warm enough for comfort. She knew that people froze to death on nights like this. But Wroxeter was not so far away, about twelve miles. If she could keep out of sight and keep moving, she might be there by morning. Perhaps to find the Black Dragon . . .

She tried to make a map in her head. A few minutes' blundering and stumbling brought her to the road that ran past the college gates, shown up by a thin glaze of starlight as a slightly lighter shade of grey in the darkness. It hadn't rained recently and the cartwheel ruts were hardened and crisped by frost.

Not a great idea to march straight past the gates like this; but she'd never be able to find her way cross-country. She could just make out the gleam of pale stone and the flash of the brass plate. The college itself was out of sight behind its thick fringe of trees. She wasn't really safe yet, but she breathed a sigh of relief as she left it behind.

Reassurance didn't last long when, not half a mile beyond the gates, she heard the sound of distant hooves. Hastily she scrambled up the steep bank by the roadside and hid behind the bulk of a tree.

The hoofbeats came nearer. And soon she could see the dull bouncing beam of a light. She held her breath. The rider came nearer, nearer.

And stopped, at the roadside just below her. The

lantern juddered to a halt and spread a faint puddle of shivering light. Fortunately she stood beyond its beam. But the rider would hear the slightest sound she made. She breathed in deeply and concentrated on stillness.

The cloaked figure was tall, and reined his horse with a masculine, military impatience. She was barely twenty feet away, and any movement, any crackle, would reveal her.

But it seemed that the stranger was not looking for her. And soon there was the sound of running footsteps and the bright lurch of another lantern. 'You got my signal,' said a female voice.

'I was watching. I thought this might happen. When did she go?'

'Just now, I think.'

The other cursed. 'They must have been waiting for her round the back. You shouldn't have let it go this far.'

'I did my best. The servant has been . . . dealt with.' The girl's voice was somehow familiar. But it wasn't until she spoke next that Livvy recognised her. 'But they managed to make contact first. At least I'm fairly sure they did.'

Of course. Lila. Big slow stupid Lila. *Oh, please just go through it with me once more, Livvy! Oh, how I wish I had a good memory like you!*

Well, that would teach her to be flattered by someone's attention. Lila who could never pass her tests, Lila who would never find a husband. Who would stay at the college for years, unnoticed except in flashes of pity and contempt from the other smarter, prettier ones. What a great cover for someone engaged on other matters.

'How do you know?'

44

'Saw them talking. And her – that Bronwen – she was jumpy all right.'

'Well, she's no danger now. Good work.'

Livvy realised that she had been holding her breath so hard that her chest was hurting. In normal circumstances you never thought about breathing out. But now it was the most important thing in her life. Breathe . . . soon . . . she'd have to or she'd burst. Breathe . . .

And suddenly an owl flew out of the tree just behind her with a huge clatter of wings. The pair jumped. Livvy let out a deep juddering breath under cover of the confusion.

The man, recognising the owl, gave a short barking laugh. 'Startled me. Keep an eye around the college; this might be a false alarm.'

'What will you do?'

'Well, we have to assume they'll make arrangements for her to join them. It might work in our favour after all. Probably she'll go to one of their mountain cells. She's deeply implicated in all this. We'll arrange a search party at first light.'

'The college probably will too.'

The man let out a snort. 'That load of virgins?'

'I'd best get back,' said Lila. 'Or they'll be looking for me too.'

'Right,' said the man, and he uttered an old military farewell followed by words Livvy didn't recognise.

'*In peace for Rome*,' replied the girl, and she turned and walked briskly back towards the college. The man waited for a few minutes, then mounted his horse with a swirl of his dark cloak and galloped off again into the night.

Livvy leaned against a tree and caught up with her breathing. She waited awhile until the quietness had reestablished itself, and then jumped down the bank and back onto the road. The jump jarred her ankle which she'd forgotten about.

More cautiously now she continued down the lane. From time to time, she came across huge carved gateposts which suggested quiet villas buried deep in the trees. The sort of area to which the wealthy retired to live out their days. Or where military commanders who'd retired from service might choose to put down roots. The man on horseback must have come from one such place, and not too far away.

But they'd got things wrong. Nobody was waiting for her 'round the back' nor was she 'deeply implicated'. Perhaps Max's wild talk had suggested this, but their information was wrong – and that was something of a relief. Maybe with any luck it would send them on a false trail.

An hour might have passed, but she couldn't see her watch. Her ankle began to hurt badly now. She wasn't sure what to do about it, so she took off her white Ishtar sash and wrapped it tightly round, fastening it with the star-pin. At least Ishtar could do her some good, she thought. The ankle seemed to hurt just as much as she continued walking, but she hoped it would swell up less.

Nervous energy kept her going. And eventually, she came to a road junction. Before her now was the main road to Wroxeter.

The surface was covered with tar and gravel and at very occasional intervals were the high lampposts which marked roadside rest-stations and cafés. She could see one such, a faint gleam on the horizon.

There was no traffic on the road now. Most long-distance or night-travellers went by steam barge anyway; you wouldn't expect many people to be around now.

She'd let the darkness shield her from the worse dangers. At least the road was straight and its destination known.

The road was ghostly pale and empty, beneath a sky riddled with stars. She kept to the verge, only scrambling to the side when she came into the glow of a way-station. Once a coach clattered by spookily, and she stood out of sight while it passed. Around her, trees, bushes and sleeping farmyards. A badger lumbered across the road in front of her, and a fox ran swiftly.

She began to feel bitterly cold and tired; she could not stop her teeth chattering and her ankle throbbing.

And eventually she was aware of the faintest silvering of the sky ahead. Dawn was breaking.


# 7


And now, she could see Wroxeter in the distance; a spreading stain on the countryside, smoke rising in dark scribbles. In her mind's eye, she pictured the main roads where the ancient gates still stood. They'd be full of people milling around, walking to work, delivering goods.

Time to leave the main road now and continue out of sight. On one side was a new development of little red houses. On the other, a straggly wood behind a dry-stone wall. She scrambled over the wall towards the wood.

She was shivering now, with exhaustion and cold and the pain of her ankle. All she wanted to do was curl up and sleep.

Suddenly there were hands on her shoulders and a voice shattering her ears. 'Gotcha!' shouted the voice.

She spun round in terror. Two large men stood there, dressed in brown woollen sweaters and trousers, woollen hats pulled over their ears. One had a chain tattooed around his bull neck. Their breath came in hot clouds as they laughed at her.

'Lost your way, *cariad?*'

'Want some help, do you?'

Frozen and worn out, her instinctive reaction was to burst into tears. Well, they'd found her now; that was the end of it. She was so cold and tired she didn't care.

But they went on talking at her. Someone told her not to cry. Huge arms pushed her forward, not ungently, into a clearing in the woods. Trees had been cut down and wagons loaded with building materials were parked around. In the middle, a brazier burned, and several more men sat around with cups of tea and sandwiches. Curious faces stared up at her.

'Look what we found in the woods,' said the man with the tattoo.

'A little lost sheep, eh?'

'Give us a *cwtsh*, then.'

'Nice and warm here, innit?'

'No need to cry, *cariad*. He won't hurt you.'

'Llew might, though. Proper animal, he is.'

'Mind, we'll look after you, won't we, boys?'

As they laughed and joshed, it began to occur to her that these men weren't the ones who were looking for her. These had the rich Cymric accents of the west; it

48

seemed that she had encountered a group of builders having their early morning break.

She was pushed nearer the fire, and someone noticed how cold she was, and that she was limping. For a moment, the joking gave way to concern. She was made to sit on a blanket and a smelly sweater put round her shoulders. '*Duw*, she's half dead with cold.' The warmth of the fire blazed up to meet her. A tin mug of steaming sweet tea was placed gently in her hands. 'There you go, girl.'

'Drink up now, before we rape you.'

'Oh, shut your big mouth, Bryn. No-one's going to hurt you, girl.'

She couldn't have fought them off, anyway. It was just nice to have the warmth of the tea and the fire taking her mind off the pain of her ankle which had suddenly become excruciating.

For a while they let her just sit there, sipping tea and warming herself. The conversation shifted and they talked of football and racing, of spending their winnings at the pub and old so-and-so getting rotten drunk.

Then the talk died away, as they studied her.

Livvy was feeling more like her old self now. In spite of the swearing that peppered their conversation and their crude jokes, these men seemed to be, more or less, harmless. She decided to confide in them, sort of. Not the real story, but an equivalent which might get their sympathy. The Cymrics of the west weren't known for their love of Roman ways.

'That's better, now, innit?' said the man with the tattoo, who seemed to be the gentlest of them. 'Going to tell us what you're up to now, are you?'

Livvy nodded and gulped the last of her tea. 'My

name's Livia,' she said, 'Livia Rheged.' Partly true –
Rheged was her mother's surname, and she thought
it would win her more sympathy than her other one,
which she had no intention of sharing with them, just in
case.

'I've run away from Ishtar College,' she said, to a
whoop of glee from the men. Everyone had heard of
Ishtar, though no-one knew much about it, just that it
was a secretive place full of strictly brought-up young
girls. Llew the big-mouth cracked a crude joke and was
silenced by the others.

'They arrange marriages for you,' she said. 'They
marry you off to these ancient blokes in the army. I
didn't want that to happen to me, so I ran away.'

Whistles of sympathy now, and a discussion of the
perfidies of the ruling classes. One or two of the men
said they wouldn't want their daughters sent to that
place, not no way.

'Where are you headed now, then?'

'Back to the city. I've got friends there who'll look
after me.'

'They'll have the search parties out now, girl.'

'I know,' she said quietly. 'I don't know how I'll get
back.'

There was buzz of conversation. 'Rhodri could . . . in
his wagon . . . got to go back anyway, soon . . . she'd be
safe in that.'

Soon they told her what they were on about. Rhodri –
who wasn't the nice one she already trusted, but a little
man with a sideways grin and big ears – had to go back
to the city that morning, to pick up a load of pipes from
a builder's yard, and could take her in the empty cart.
They'd hide her under a tarpaulin, and that way, she'd

get through the dangerous entry to the city, at least. From there, she'd have to make her own way but once she was inside the city, she could just mingle with the crowds.

Well, she wasn't sure if she could trust weaselly little Rhodri but she had no choice. 'Thanks,' she said. 'I'd really appreciate that.'

While she was waiting, they gave her a bacon sandwich for her breakfast, which she gulped down greedily. She received several proposals of marriage while she was eating and several proposals for other things. But it was all amiable.

So a short while later, she was lying under a bench in a wagon, hidden by a tarpaulin, rumbling and lurching towards what she sincerely hoped was the city.

She dozed on and off intermittently so she had no idea how long the journey took. From time to time Rhodri asked her if she was all right; from time to time she heard him talking to other drivers.

Gradually the noises of the city increased around her, and its familiar smell, dung and smoke and bad drains. There was a lurch around a corner, and she heard Rhodri calling the horse to a halt. Then he said, 'You can come out now.'

She pulled the tarpaulin off and scrambled out, her limbs stiff and her ankle so sore she could hardly stand on it. She didn't want Rhodri fussing round her, though, so she tried to disguise her pain. He had taken her cautiously into an empty road with warehouses on one side and a blank wall on the other. She recognised the area of the city vaguely – an industrial zone just near the old city walls.

'You be all right now?' he asked. She nodded.

'Just as well you hid,' he said. 'There was these military types stood by the gate. Dead suspicious. Reckon you had a lucky escape, little Miss Ishtar.'

'I did. Thanks.'

He looked hopefully at her. 'We could go somewhere if you like. I know this place. No-one'd know . . .'

Her stomach lurched. Was she going to have to fend him off? She shook her head hard. 'No. Please. No.'

But to her relief, he simply shrugged and said, 'Whatever.' She thanked him again and they parted. There were decent people in the world after all.

As she set off, her ankle seemed to settle down to a low ache that was just about tolerable. She came out of the quiet street into another row of warehouses and around the corner from that into a district of small businesses, builders' yards, nursery gardens, blacksmiths and wheelwrights. She pulled her blanket around her head and hurried purposefully, not looking around her. The break had restored her energy, which was just as well, for she knew it would take the best part of an hour to reach the docks by the canal.

The city was busy first thing, workmen and housemaids hurrying to their jobs. Patricians would be around a bit later. The army and Military Police were in evidence as usual, climbing out of army vehicles, standing on street corners, striding along as though they owned the city – which in many ways of course, they did. She just had to pray that not every soldier would be looking for her.

As she crossed through the street markets just setting up their array of winter vegetables, the workmen's cafés smelling of hot coffee and bacon fat, she tried to put together all the information she had gathered about what was happening to her. It wasn't much. Max was obviously mixed up in something – perhaps it was the group everyone called *Bleiddiaid* – the Wolves. That wasn't what they were really called, just what the papers had dreamed up for them and the name had stuck. Their aims were unclear to the general run of citizens – just that they were something to do with destabilizing imperial power. As well as the riots, there'd been random bombings and terrorist attacks on steam barges carrying passengers over the last years. Of course, there could have been some other secret group at work, but as people said, who else would want to stir up trouble, if it wasn't the *Bleidiaidd*? Livvy wasn't too sure that she approved of them either. Her father certainly didn't – although he had things to criticise about the army, he hated terrorists even more.

But she still couldn't understand why the army was so keen to find her.

She reached the smart shopping boulevard. The street bisected the old city centre. On one side, the huge half-ruined building which used to be the Basilica in ancient days. Now restored, with trees and shrubs planted around, old stonework patched up with new, it was a museum, famous as the place where the young went to chat each other up without parents getting suspicious. Beyond the museum, on a road straight as a knife, and elegantly wide, were the shops, massive buildings of ornately carved stone. Their windows glittered with beautiful things, fabrics and furnishings, jewellery and clothes. Trees lined the road, and at night, big round globes glowed from tall iron lampstands. How often she'd wandered here with her mother, window shopping, chatting to acquaintances or having tea and cakes in elegant little cafés that spilled on to the pavements. It all seemed like another world now.

A friend of her mother's who lived in one of the fashionable apartments above the shops came past now, swathed in furs, a little white dog on a lead. Livvy froze in horror, but the woman sailed straight past her. As an ordinary girl wrapped in an old blanket, she'd become invisible.

And here, overlooking the little park, was the block of flats where her grandmother had lived in a rambling apartment full of heavy old-lady furniture – *Nain* as Livvy still liked to call her, though her mother didn't approve of that. Nain had belonged to a local group that was passionate about everything Cymric. Livvy remembered the slightly eccentric but amusing people who'd passed through the flat, all enthusiastically talking the old language. Livvy's mother refused to have anything to do with that side of her ancestry, and made sure she was as Roman as could be, but Livvy had been very fond of Nain, even her eccentricities, and had loved hearing the old stories of Bran the Blessed, and the Birds of Rhiannon. She wondered who lived in Nain's old flat now and what had happened to those eager members of *Cymdeithas Caer Gurion,* the Wroxeter Cymric Society. No sign of any friendly faces today.

Livvy felt safer when she'd passed through the shopping quarter. A series of streets, increasingly dingy, massed with bulky windowless buildings, led to the waterways. And before too long, she could see it at the end of the road, the great canal, built by slaves two hundred years ago, wide and deep as a river, with the steam barges and dockyards, the little ferries and the cranes and the loading-wagons on metal tracks.

But as she was about to come out of the dark street which led on to the dockside, a clatter of activity stopped her. She pulled herself back into a dark archway, to see a group of Military Police in their black and silver uniforms, barking out commands to passers-by and manual workers.

# 8

Livvy waited a long while in the dark archway. Then she back-tracked and took another turning. There was a row of small and dingy shops – a second-hand clothes shop, a shoe-repairers and the inevitable workmen's café.

She'd nearly walked past this last place, when just by luck she looked up at the peeling sign that hung there. The Black Dragon.

So she took a deep breath and walked straight in, into the greasy steam of the café. Men sat round shovelling stews and fry-ups into their mouths. No-one took much notice of her. She waited in a queue, at a counter where a man in a grubby striped apron dispensed tea from a huge urn. Limp sandwiches and flattened buns wilted under glass domes.

'Yes?' barked the man, when it was Livvy's turn. Several men now stood behind her.

She had no idea what to say, who to ask for. 'I want to see someone, please,' she said, conscious of her clear, well-bred accent. The man looked at her for a moment. He had an angular dark face with eyes and mouth pulled down disagreeably.

'Who do you want to see?' he snapped.

'I don't know. I . . .' Livvy hesitated.

The man made an impatient face, but his eyes flickered briefly. He squirted steaming tea into a cup and shoved it in front of her, gesturing with a flick of his head that she was to take a seat.

She went to sit down, perched at the corner of a table where two men, wiping greasy plates with bread, talked about last night's dog-fighting. The thought of dog-fights made Livvy feel sick, even through her nervousness. She sipped her tea.

She had not got to the end of the cup, however, when suddenly the door was flung open. Tables moved and crashed; chairs were toppled. Into the café marched a group of Military Police, guns cradled at the ready.

Everything happened so fast. Before any of the startled customers could move, the soldiers reached the counter. They pinioned the man at the tea-urn. Then the woman who'd been wiping plates in the back. She screamed; she swore; plates went crashing.

A soldier swivelled round to face the customers, gun pointing. Livvy felt a stomach-churning surge of fear.

He menaced them for a few moments, raking them over with hard eyes, the gun barrel glinting. Then he said, 'No, we don't want you lot. Out, all of you.'

People were hesitant, immobilised by fear. 'NOW!!' he shouted. Oh, the power of the gun. At once, there was a mad scramble to get out of the café. Livvy scrambled as much as any of them, pushing and shoving.

Outside, some of the men ran off; others gathered in little shocked groups. Livvy, after a moment's gasping for breath, ran off too, into the network of dark streets and vaulted tunnels.

She paused, in the dark damp space beneath a bridge,

water dripping down slimed and sodden brickwork. This time she'd been lucky; it wasn't her they'd been looking for. No doubt they were after Max and his friends, who used the Black Dragon. A few minutes later, and they might have picked her up too.

But where to now? She didn't have a friend here.

Unless . . .

For she remembered who else lived in this dingy area.

She'd been to his apartment once or twice before, with her friends, on occasions when a particularly bad hangover had kept him from opening up the school. Loyalty to Don was a tradition among the girls of Sixth Precinct. She doubted that any of them had told their parents of the lengths they used to go to to keep their teacher among them.

Soon she had found the road where Don had his apartment. Half the shops here were boarded up or vandalised. Don lived between a barber's shop and a gloomy old pub – she remembered that, because the girls used to laugh at the name: the Minerva's Owl – as if any of the regulars cared for the goddess of Wisdom here. Except for Don, of course.

He lived on the third floor of a blackish-red building. An open communal staircase led up through piles of rubbish, stinking with urine. An angry-looking dog rushed out from somewhere and barked at her. Livvy paused for a moment, and said, 'Good boy! Back!' in what she hoped was a confident voice.

The door to Don's apartment was locked, but that was no problem, because they knew where he kept the key – under a plant pot with a dead geranium. As she pushed open the door, the broken pane of stained glass rattled.

She went into a dark hallway. A blast of musty air met her and a strong smell of whisky. But nothing worse than that. Don was clean enough when he was sober to make up for the times when he was too drunk to care.

She pushed open the door to the living room. Through half-shut blinds, a thin yellowish light drizzled onto walls covered with bookshelves. On an old sofa covered with a cream cotton cover, Don sat, or rather half sprawled. He was wearing a stained vest and dark trousers. His round, ruddy face was thrown back against the cushion, his small blue eyes were half closed, and – she could see in the semi-darkness – very red. His face reminded her for some reason of a round, flattened football – if a football can have sprouting gingery hair.

He knew somebody had come in, but she could tell he was pretending not to notice. Then he screwed his eyes tight shut, cursed and swore copiously, and said, 'All right! All right! What do you want now?'

He struggled to a sitting position. 'Why are you hounding me? It's no a school day today.' Then he saw who it was. He sat up straight. 'Jove's bollocks, lassie. It's you. What are you doing here?'

'Hello, Don,' she said.

'We thought you were . . . Well, dead was what we thought, if you must know. Ouch. Oh my head. I'm not up to this.'

'I'll make you some coffee,' she said. A practised routine. She'd done this before for him, and in his apartment too.

The little kitchen was spartan. Very little sign that Don did much eating. She found the kettle and put it on the range. There was a tin of coffee and she spooned some into a jug. She also sliced bread from a stale loaf,

58

and found some cheese. While the kettle boiled, she toasted the bread and the cheese. The smell of food made her feel slightly queasy, and would probably do the same for Don. But if he'd been on a weekend binge, he probably hadn't eaten for days.

He glowered at her as she carried the tray in: strong sweet black coffee in a tin mug, a hunk of cheese on toast.

'Oh, but you lasses torment me,' he said. 'All right now. Tell me what happened to you.'

'Have your coffee first,' she said. 'I'm in trouble. You'll need a strong head.'

'You're in trouble?' he said. 'Not . . .?'

'No, not that kind of trouble, silly. I'll tell you.'

And she did, the whole story, from Max's two messages, her time in Ishtar, the episode with the girl Bronwen, her own escape, the people who seemed to be looking for her.

The story took a long time to tell. When she'd finished, Don said, 'This coffee's cold.'

'Do you want some more?'

'Yes,' he said. 'Stronger this time.'

So she made more coffee. When she came back with the mug, he said, 'You had us worried there. Helen went round to your house the other day. It was shut up, everyone gone. She spoke to next door's servants. The mistress's been sent to a hospital, they said. Servants dismissed. All of them.'

A hospital? A nice, gentle Ishtarian hospital, no doubt, for people with addiction problems . . .

And all the servants – Minna, Llew, Catti, who'd been with them for years – where were they all now?

'It's worse than I thought,' she said. 'Oh, Don, what'll I do?'

'Don't know why you ask me that,' he said. 'I never passed my hero test. Or my quick-thinking-in-a-crisis test, come to that.'

'There's no-one else I can ask.'

'I don't know anything,' he said. 'At least . . .'

'At least what?'

He drained his coffee in one gulp. 'Fetch me some paper. There. On the desk. And a pencil. Now. What does this mean to you?'

She stared at the scribbled shape. 'A Greek letter.'

'Which one?'

'Theta.'

'And . . .?'

'The eighth letter of the Greek alphabet. Actually, I've seen that somewhere recently. I don't know . . .'

'Well, I'll tell you a little story. It doesn't have an end, this story, so don't expect too much from it. A few years ago, I wanted to write a book, about all these weird religions that people are getting mixed up in these days. My theory, for what's it's worth, is that our old Empire is breaking down, and when that happens, people turn to the gods, lots of them, the dafter the better.'

'Go on.'

'I suppose it got out, what I was up to. I wasn't being especially secretive. Well, one day a strange fellow comes to see me, in the pub. He was tanned like old leather, covered in scars. A real old soldier. Said he had something to tell me. Something explosive. He wanted to meet me. Another pub, another night. I said, give me some idea of what you're about. He reached down, and just drew that shape out of the beer ring on the table. Theta. All right, so I arranged to meet him. I turned up; he didn't.'

'So?'

'I told you, lassie, the story doesn't have an end. Except that he, my old soldier, was stabbed in an alleyway that evening. A mate of mine saw the body being carted off. From how he described him, it was my man all right.'

'What did you do?'

'I told you, Livia, I'm no hero. But I asked around. Army fellows. All went very quiet on me, especially when I mentioned Theta. But one said, I'd find the answer in the temple of Sol Invicta, in London.'

'Sol Invicta – the Unconquered Sun – that's one of Mithras's names. What happened to the book?'

'Oh, I'll finish it one day, I don't doubt. But I received the definite impression that I was on perilous ground.'

'And that's all?'

'Well, except for what I could put together myself. What do you know about Mithras, girl?'

'Not a lot. I can tell you loads about Ishtar though.'

'Girl's stuff. Rubbish.'

'Well, my brother's mad about Mithras. But he won't tell you anything. It's all secrets.'

'You know some things.'

'Well, I know there are seven levels, just like in Ishtar. Only it's much more serious and it all takes longer. The Ishtar Levels are called after colours, the Mithras Levels are named after the Greek alphabet.'

'Exactly.'

'But there are only seven levels. Theta is the eighth letter.'

'Exactly, too.'

'But so what?'

61

'So what, means I don't know. But if the Empire's growing old and dozy then the next big thing is waiting in the shadows to pounce. And there's something else I've heard, in the pubs near the docks, from sailors coming over from Gaul. The Emperor's ill. Terminal cancer. They're trying to hush it up, but they can't for ever. He hasn't got long now. And then what?'

'What do you mean?'

'Something's building up, that's all I can say.'

Livvy tried to take it all in. 'So what can I do?'

'I don't think you're safe here.'

'Where can I go, though?'

'Hmm,' he said. 'Interesting. I'll think about it. I know. I can send you to Lena. She's my cousin. A bit peculiar, but she'd look after you. Nobody'd make the connection with you there.'

'Where does she live?'

'London.'

'London! I can't travel to London. I haven't got the papers, for one thing.'

'Papers, aye, papers. We'll just have to see what we can do.'

'And suppose they're looking for me at the docks?'

'They'll be looking for a lassie in a blue dress, won't they?'

'I guess.'

'Well, just suppose you were someone else. Let's see. You're quite tall, quite slim. Hmm. Ever thought of having your hair cut?'

'Don, what are you on about?'

'I tell you, I've got friends in low places. Now you wait here for me. I'll be back as soon as I can.'

# 9

The winter sky was stained deep purple by the lights of the city, almost drowning the stars. The water in the canal glimmered and shimmered. The great London-bound steamer, *Marcus Aurelius,* loomed up at the quay-side, lights blazing. It was due to leave at midnight; engines growling and panting, steam coming in little gasps from the funnels. Most people had boarded by now, but a group of aristocrats, fashionably late, laughed as they made their ways to the gangplank from the ticket office. The women were swathed in furs, the men in heavy dark overcoats.

Also at the ticket office was a thin boy, dressed in brown woollen workmen's clothes, a pull-on hat, soft serge trousers and a greasy sheepskin jerkin. He jumped from foot to foot, shivery and nervous. An inspector, doing a routine inspection, asked to see his papers. The boy pulled a scruffy bundle from his pocket, and the inspector noted his details: Glyn Howells, age thirteen, resident of London, just finished six weeks' temporary employment in the tin foundries.

The inspector handed back the papers. 'You're wasting your time standing around here, though.'

'What do you mean?' said the boy, in a kind of croak.

'She's full tonight. Steerage is full, anyway.'

'But they got on.'

'They're first class, lad. Not for the likes of you. Come along now.'

And young Glyn Howells found himself being pushed back, away from the great steamer. He protested loudly for a while – he had to get to London tonight – but the inspector wasn't interested.

Glyn Howells sank down on a bench and sunk his head in his hands. Almost as if – how unmanly – the lad was going to cry.

'London, did you say?'

Glyn Howells looked up. A boy stood there. He was about sixteen, seventeen. His dark hair was shaven close; he had a narrow band tattooed around his brow, and another on his wrist. He wore thick grey woollen clothes, a heavy sweater and boots.

'Only we're off to London. Over there.'

He nodded in the direction of an old barge, also moored by the quayside.

'The *Diligence*. Not as glamorous as the *Marcus A,* but she'll get you there. Cost you though, mind.'

'I've got money. Some, anyway.'

'Loading and unloading's more what I had in mind. My dad's done his back in, and my uncle refuses to lift anything. I could do with the help.'

'I'm not,' said Glyn Howells tremulously, 'much of a sailor.'

'Oh, come on,' said the boy. 'Live dangerously, why not?'

Glyn knew he was being laughed at, but pulled together the shreds of his dignity to reply. 'All right then.'

The boy held out a hand. 'Cai Llewelyn.'

'Glyn. Glyn Howells.'

Cai Llewelyn gave him an odd look. 'All right then. I'm just off to get a sandwich. See you on board, ten minutes.'

*Marcus Aurelius* moved away, with a triumphant blast of her deep hooters, down the canal, in a glory of glittering lights. 'A beaut, isn't she?' said Cai. 'Promised

64

myself I'll go on her one of these days. Anyway, come on, we've loads more bales to get into the hold.'

The *Diligence* was moored by the quayside, a squat and stumpy little steamer that had seen better days. Bales of woollen fabric wrapped in oilcloth, crates of china and various trunks and boxes were to be loaded into her capacious but cramped belly. Glyn Howells struggled as he hefted the stuff on board. Some of it he could barely lift. The other boy shouldered the bales effortlessly and ran up the gangplank with them. All around came the sounds of night, sounds that a respectable girl would never hear: sailors yelling, every other word an obscenity, drunks singing, men quarrelling. Oil lamps swung from posts, painting everything in garish intense colours, carving faces into deep shadows. From time to time, Cai had to chivvy along his new crew member, unaccountably fascinated by the whole show.

At one o'clock Cai's father and uncle staggered in from the pub, clutching bottles of beer, packs of sandwiches and an evening paper. They were small wiry men, sunburned, close shaven, their bodies and foreheads a mass of half-faded old tattoos. Neither spoke much, except in grunts and curses.

Cai's father peered at Glyn. 'What's he doing?'

Cai was unperturbed. 'Giving me a hand. Since you can't.'

'Well, he's given you a hand. Now he can push off.'

'He's coming to London,' said Cai.

'He's not eating my bloody food all the way to London.'

'No,' said Cai. 'He's not eating your bloody food. He's eating my bloody food.' He winked at Glyn, who smiled weakly.

'Can he cook?' the uncle said. 'We could use a cook.'

Livvy wondered how long she was going to be able to keep this up. She had hardly ever been in the kitchen, except to make the odd snack. Nice girls didn't cook of course. That's what servants were for. But she was beginning to learn just how useless were the life-skills she'd acquired so painstakingly and expensively over the years. 'No. I can't cook. Sorry.'

Cai's uncle snorted and shoved the evening paper onto the table. The little cabin was cramped and hot and smelly, just a table and four benches around it. 'Well then, shut up,' he said. 'I need my beauty sleep.'

He stretched out on the bench, kicking a guitar case out of the way. Cai picked it up with a sigh and stowed it away carefully. 'We leave at dawn,' he said. 'Get a bit of rest while you can, Glyn.'

Cai and his dad each took one of the benches and sprawled out. The room smelt of beer and sweat and old wool. Livvy scrambled on to a bench and stretched out too. Her head felt hot and achy and her stomach was churning. Only a day or so ago she'd been in the refined company of young girls and ladies, and here she was surrounded by three sweaty, snoring men. All the thoughts of what could happen to her crowded into her overexcited brain. She'd never sleep! How could she relax here?

But then, someone was shaking her; she was cold and stiff and dreams were racing away out of her head – amazingly she'd slept, and slept heavily too. She sat up bemused while things were going on all around her. Cai shoved a mug of hot tea in front of her. 'Need the toilet,' she muttered in embarrassment, and he grinned and showed her which door it was. The toilet was cramped and smelly and didn't have a lock. She braced her foot against the door while she used it.

When she emerged, everything was in chaos. Cai cooked beans over a little oil stove, while one of the men shaved at a small mirror on the table. Cai's father was pulling on thick sweaters and boots, while his uncle was stripped to his vest. She soon realised why: the uncle – Ifan – was off to stoke the boiler whereas the father – Dai – would be in the wheelhouse on deck.

Cai put a plate of beans before her. 'Just keep your head down and they won't notice you,' he hissed. 'We stop at Leicester – you can give me a hand then.' She wondered why he was being so nice to her – she was pretty useless here after all.

She sat there as the barge came to life around her: loud avalanches of coal as the boiler was filled, and then the gasping of the heated steam, the rattle of chains, assorted crashes and bangs and swearing, and then eventually the chugging of the engine as it warmed into life and the boat began to lurch and move, the perpetual running of footsteps up and down. All this time she'd kept absolutely still as Cai had suggested, sitting hunched on the bench, hugging her knees as if she could make herself invisible.

But then, after an hour or so, things seemed to have calmed down, and the boat settled to a steady chug. She longed to go on deck, to watch what was going on, but she didn't quite dare.

Instead, she reached out for last night's evening paper that still lay on the table stained with rings of tea. It was folded over and she could see only half a blurred photo and some print.

Then she opened it out. The photo unfolded into

something heart-stoppingly familiar and the headline leaped out at her.

## MURDER SUSPECT SLAIN IN CAFÉ SHOOTOUT

She was shaking so much that she had to read the paragraph several times over, and even then it didn't make sense. Max's photo – she recognised it as one taken around the time of his fourteenth birthday – grinned out cheekily at her, his spiky hair sticking up jauntily.

*Military Police announced another success in the fight against terrorism, when they carried out an early morning raid on a dockland premises known for some time to have sheltered a terrorist cell. At the Black Dragon café, several suspects were seized and taken into custody. Another suspect, Max Madoc, 16, wanted for the brutal murder of Commander Justin Lucas in November, was shot while resisting arrest. Police say that with his death, the file on Commander Lucas's killing is now closed. 'Madoc was a brutal and ruthless killer,' said Inspector Collis this lunchtime. 'The citizens of our city can now sleep more safely in their beds . . .'*

At first the shock was numbing, but then after the numbness, emotions came in a rush. Chief among them was panic and an overwhelming urge to burst into tears, which she did, crying silently into her folded arms. Yet even as she wept helplessly, something angry and fierce was building up inside her. *This isn't right,* she thought, *Max was never a killer, and somebody – more than one somebody – knows it too. Something terribly wrong is going on and this is only a part of it. I need to know what it is, because otherwise how can I get myself out of it?*

She wiped her eyes, and sat still, her eyes dry now, unblinking, trying to concentrate. There was a jigsaw of scattered facts that needed assembling, but she couldn't put them together. Instead a scene played itself in her mind – Max the last time she'd seen him. It had been about six months ago; before that, they hadn't met for almost a year. Max, whose relations with his mother were worsening, had been packed off for a long stay with his father's relatives in the Cymric west. (So that she could carry on her affairs with half the officers in the barracks, Max had claimed bitterly.) Things were different there – different and freer. Long ago, in those dark years when Rome was busy dealing with invaders from the east, the princes of the west had taken advantage, and had established strong and independent kingdoms. With the Empire securely established again, Rome had tried to drag the Cymrics back to heel. After centuries of war, an uneasy compromise was reached – West Cymru, ruled by a Council, overseen by a Rome-appointed Prefect, was granted a degree of independence, as long as it provided the Empire lavishly with choice goods, cattle, woollen cloth and silver, but most of all, soldiers, the famous Cymric archers. The land was so poor that Rome wasn't too interested anyway.

Though all that had changed thirty years ago as the Steam Age was getting underway, and they found that the quiet valleys of the south were stuffed with desirable coal. That was one of the reasons for the *Bleidiaidd*, who wanted to keep their assets from passing into the greedy maw of the Empire. Times were changing, but the freedoms were still there, and for someone like Max it was intoxicating.

Max had gone reluctantly, but had come back transformed, full of new enthusiasms. He and Livvy had sneaked off to one of their old dockside haunts, though they were very different from the children they'd used to be. Max had grown up – in that strange lurching way that boys grew, not by gradual transition, as did girls, but in uncomfortable leaps and starts, so that his voice and his body seemed to belong to half a dozen different Maxes: his limbs were ungainly; his feet were huge; his voice cracked and growled weirdly. But he'd been talking in the same old excited way, a firework-burst of words. She only half listened to most of it, but from time to time, something made her sit up. 'Max!' she'd said at one point. 'Surely you aren't getting involved with terrorists!'

'But that's just it, don't you see?' he'd insisted. 'That's just what *they* want you to think. These people aren't terrorists. All they want, Liv, is freedom for our land.'

'What's this "our land" business?' she'd said, a little sourly. All these shadowy 'theys' were getting her down. 'Last year you wanted to join the Roman army, now you've suddenly gone all Cymric.'

'I've always been Cymric,' he insisted. 'So have you. I think that's one of the reasons they're out to get us.'

'Max,' she said wearily. 'Who is "out to get us"?'

'The people who murdered my father, of course.'

'We don't know your father was murdered. Anyway, who'd do that? The army wouldn't have murdered him. He was really popular.'

'I don't know who did it,' he'd said stubbornly. 'But I

intend to find out. And you'd better be careful. We're in this together.'

She'd stopped arguing at that point. It all seemed so stupid. But then there was the Spread Eagle. Max was too young to drink in a pub, but this was an army pub, and army pubs had their own rules. Max, for all his swagger, still had friends in the army, men who'd been good to him after his father's death, and whom he looked up to. What had he been saying to everyone? Loose talk about his father's death would have been dangerous all right, but supposing he'd given the impression that Livia was also involved?

So maybe she had Max to thank for this mess she was in. But on the other hand, maybe it was due to Max that she'd survived so long. If they – those shadowy 'theys' again – hadn't thought that she had useful information, they might have 'eliminated' her straight away. Like they'd managed to do with Max.

But she was still here. And she wanted it to stay that way. She must have been sitting there for some time when the cabin door opened and Cai came in. 'They're gagging for tea up there,' he said. 'If you were any use, you'd make it.' But he put the kettle on, and whistled an inconsequential little tune while it boiled. Livvy was too intent on her thoughts to notice him staring at her.

He made the tea, and took tin mugs out to his father and uncle. Then he came back into the cabin. He poured two more mugs, spooned an inordinate amount of sugar into one, and plonked them both down on the table, still whistling his silly song.

Then he sat down next to her on the bench. He said nothing for a while, and then: 'So OK, what's all this about?'

71

She looked up at him. 'What do you mean?'

'You make a crap bloke,' he said. 'Still, if it's any consolation, the other two don't seem to have sussed you yet.'

Livvy gave a sigh. 'How did you guess?'

'Oh, come on! I'm not daft. Plus, blokes don't pee with the door shut and the seat down. You aren't a pleb and you aren't a bloke. I have to say, it didn't take long to work it out. And anyway, I saw that piece in the paper.'

'You won't give me away, will you?'

'No reason why I should. But I want to know what all this is about.'

'It's a long story.'

'They're busy. We're an hour away from the next lock. Try me.'

She looked at him. The tattoo wound around his forehead, a narrow band of elaborate twining. She'd never been so close to a tattoo before. Or to a boy from the plebs, for that matter. She found his presence oddly disconcerting, in a way she didn't quite understand. His close-cropped hair was chestnut-brown, and his skin was tanned from the sun. Muscles and sinews in his arms spoke of physical labour, but he moved deftly and with grace and his hands were sensitive. And as far as she could tell, his face was friendly.

But what did she know? She'd thought the whole world was friendly until a month or so ago.

He picked up the newspaper which she'd flung to the floor. Carefully he reassembled the leaves and folded it back so that the face of Max stared out at them.

'He was my friend,' she said sullenly. 'They shouldn't have killed him. He didn't murder the Commander.'

Cai blinked for a moment. If she'd looked at him,

she'd have noticed that he looked surprised. This wasn't the reaction he'd expected.

'They shot your friend? The Military Police? No wonder you'd been crying.'

She nodded. 'They'd framed him for that murder. He never did it. And now he's dead, they don't have to prove it. Because they couldn't.'

'They can prove anything if they want to,' he said with surprising bitterness. 'Welcome to the real world, Glyn Howells. What's your proper name, anyway?'

She thought about all the alternatives. But somehow she couldn't cope with yet another dissembling. 'Livia,' she said. 'I'm Livia.'

'Livia,' he said. Then, 'OK, Livia Marcel. Look, when I mentioned the bit in the paper, I wasn't talking about the front page.'

She sat up. 'What do you mean?'

'You haven't seen it, have you?' He took the paper from her and riffled through it. Then he found a small paragraph on the fourth page and shoved it towards her. 'Well?'

The headline was smaller and the paragraph was tucked away. **GIRL MISSING** the headline said.

*The Headmistress of Ishtar College, Mother Elana, today appealed to the public for information about the whereabouts of a missing pupil. Livia Marcel, 15, was found to be missing from the college last night. 'She is a vulnerable pupil, who has had some problems,' said Mother Elana. 'We appeal to anybody who has knowledge of her or who may be sheltering her to come forward as soon as possible. We are most concerned for Livia's safety.'*

'Well?' repeated Cai.

Livvy was quiet for a while. 'Can I trust you?' she said.

'You got any choice?'

'Not really.' And so for the second time in as many days, she found herself telling her story.


# 10

'So where are you going to stay in London?' asked Cai when she'd finished. Seeing her hesitate, he said, 'In for a penny, girl. You've told me so much you may as well finish it off now.'

'I've just got an address. My mad teacher's mad cousin. He says I can stay there for a bit.'

'Then what?'

'I don't know.'

'You can't hide forever. These people have long memories.'

'These people!' she said. 'I don't even know who they are. If I knew, it might be easier.'

'Well, I guess the Muck aren't your best mates, just at the moment, are they?'

'The what?'

'The Muck. The Scum, the Scabs, the Pigs. The Military Police, girl.'

'Oh,' she said weakly. She'd been an army girl all her life. As a child she would run happily around her father's camp, and big smiling men in uniform would lift her up onto their horses, or into their armoured vehicles. Soldiers were her friends. It was hard to think of them as the enemy. She didn't even know the rude names.

'If it's any consolation, they aren't mine either,' he said. 'They killed my brother, didn't they?'

'*Killed?*'

'These aren't nice guys, Livia. Yeah, they killed him.'

'What happened?'

'Well, it was two years ago. Bran, my big brother, he wasn't like me. I don't have theories about things; I don't want to change the world. I just want to do my music and be left alone. But Bran was always into politics and how things were. Unfair, everything was unfair. Anyway, he got caught up with the Wolves. Like your friend Max, I guess. Well, one day he was arrested after a meeting and taken into custody. He never came out again.'

'What happened?'

'Natural causes, they said. A sudden heart attack, resisting arrest. He was sixteen, for Jove's sake.'

'I'm sorry.'

'When – eventually – they let us see his body and we had to grovel for that – it was covered in bruises. His eyes were all mashed up. Natural causes, my arse.'

He gave a deep sigh. Then he said, 'Come on, Livia Marcel. We'll be in Leicester any time now. Make sure you have your papers handy. And when they check them, just stay cool. They'll give you a hard time – they always do. But it's not personal. Don't get riled, OK?'

'I'm not used to having papers checked.'

'You'd better get used to it, then. And after that, we've got half a ton of garden ornaments to load up. You don't get away without doing your share, miss.'

It was hard work, loading up the stuff, and her arm muscles ached. The Military Police had been thorough,

75

as Cai had warned her, and had questioned her closely –
was she licensed for river work, did she intend to return
to Wroxeter? She replied as best she could – no, she
wasn't licensed for river work; she was just earning her
passage back to London, where she intended to stay for
the foreseeable future. Plebs were allowed to leave their
own zones, provided they could vouch for employment,
for a certain period. It wasn't quite as bad as the slavery
in the olden days, but freedom was restricted for the
poor. Being an upper-class girl, and from a military
family at that, Livvy had never known these sorts of
restrictions. Probably the restrictions were there
underneath, but they were so gentle, so unobtrusive that
she'd never been aware of them.

She thought of the last time she'd travelled to
London. It must had been three or four years ago now –
her father was still alive, and her mother hadn't yet sunk
into her chemical-fuelled dream world. They'd gone up
by road, in a smart, well-sprung military carriage, staying
at the best hotels on the way. They stayed with her
father's old friend, Commander Gregory Flavian. What
she remembered of London was broad tree-lined
boulevards, elegant squares with their white stucco
mansions and well-kept gardens, huge vistas closing in
triumphal arches or equestrian statues of famous
generals. It was a great time for their family – Father was
to receive his Military Cross from the Governor. They'd
stayed for a week with Commander Flavian, with
Priscilla, his wife, and Julia and Clare, their daughters.
The girls seemed so old and sophisticated – though Clare
must have been the same age that Livvy was now – with
their talk of boys and stage stars and clothes and make-
up. Priscilla – Aunt Priscilla, she'd called her, though she

wasn't a real aunt – was fashionable, gracious and charming. The child Livvy had seen nothing to dislike in her, though the older Livvy looking back, sensed that now she wouldn't like her so much. But 'Uncle' Gregory had been one of her father's oldest friends, along with Max's father. The three of them had trained together at the Military Academy and gone on their first campaigns together. Commander Flavian had even been on the campaign in which her father had won his medal. Livvy's own father had been quiet and a little reserved until you got to know him; Max's father 'Uncle' Paul had been like Max himself, wild and not quite predictable, full of silly jokes. People said later that this was just another side of the depression that must have killed him, the sudden unexpected suicide. But Uncle Gregory was different again. He had the authentic old Roman look – thick dark hair and dark eyes and a big 'Roman' nose. He was always smiling and looked at you as though he was listening to everything you said. Although Max, when he was going through one of his paranoid-about-everything phases, once said he didn't really think Commander Flavian ever *listened* to anything you said – he just looked as though he did.

Livvy had enjoyed her stay there, the large and glamorous house with real electric lights, the attentive servants and the grandeur of London. The award ceremony had been held in the Governor's palace, and that had been an experience in itself, the Imperial Guard in their dress uniform of red and gold, the frocks and hats of the ladies, the military music, the meticulous movements of the beautifully-drilled soldiers – nowhere in the world could you find an army as well drilled as in the Empire, Livvy's father said proudly. It had been nice too, having her father recognised as a hero and hearing again the story of how he'd rescued three of his men in the face of appalling enemy fire in the Macedonian Campaigns. It occurred to her to wonder why she hadn't thought of turning up on Aunt Priscilla and Uncle Gregory's doorstep, asking for their support in this horrible time. But it hadn't occurred to her, and now that it did, something held her back from asking them. She didn't know what that something was, but it just gnawed uneasily at her.

In the meantime she was learning all sorts of things about boats. She knew what the ropes were called; she could tell port from starboard, and even knew how to work the locks. Cai helped her when he remembered but he was busy too, helping his uncle and father, sometimes – though he was officially too young to do so – even taking a turn at the wheel. That next evening, they found a mooring not far from Towcester, and Cai bought cheese sandwiches from a fast food stall. Though the sandwiches were rough and greasy, Livvy was starving and they tasted good. To her relief the father and uncle went off to the pub. Most of the day they'd ignored her, but they'd taken to calling her 'the young lady' – not because they saw through her disguise but because they saw an effeminate boy. If they'd looked a bit harder, they might have sussed her, but fortunately neither seemed to be the observant type.

In the peace of the cabin Cai took up his guitar and played. He played folk songs and some of the popular music that Livvy loved but was never officially allowed to listen to (the girls of Sixth Precinct had to buy sheet music and try out the tunes on the tinny old school piano at lunch time, dreaming about being allowed one day to go to the clubs and bars where the real thing was played). Cai was good. He played well, and his voice sent shivers down her spine. She knew so few boys – there was Tony, who didn't count, but he had been a pain in the neck for as long as she could remember. And Max, of course, who had been like a brother. Cai was different from both, funnier and sharper than Tony, but calmer and slower than Max. His sense of humour was slow-burning rather than manic. And he seemed kind. Could she trust him? She wanted to think so. And anyway, just at the moment, she had no choice.

Later, the men came back from the pub, and things got noisy again. Livvy heard jokes she would never have heard as a young lady and learned some interesting new words. Cai gave her a sideways grin from time to time, hoping probably she'd be embarrassed, so even when she was, she assumed a calm heard-it-all-before manner. She was dreading another night spent in the smelly cabin, but Cai found her a quiet place to sleep in a store cabin, on a pile of musty blankets, and once more she slept through the night, her muscles aching pleasantly from the work she'd done.

The following morning, they were up again in the cold dawn. A quick cup of tea and then more things to be loaded and unloaded – the garden ornaments were going, and sacks of building materials were coming. Cai let her use a barrow and that way she could get them up the gangplank, though the men thought that most amusing. Then they started off again, along the misty waterway, the sound of the engine filling her ears, her eyes watering from the cold. She watched fields and trees unfolding past her. They passed through smoky little red-brick towns and calm villages, through factories and estates and farms. Road bridges arched over the canal; rivers sometimes looped close. She couldn't imagine a better way of travelling.

'Breakfast'd be good,' said Cai's uncle, suddenly, cutting into her reverie.

Cai sighed, 'I'll get it.'

'No,' said Livvy quickly. 'I will.'

He gave her a quizzical look, but said nothing. Livvy regretted it almost at once, but she wasn't about to retract. So she dodged down the narrow steps and into the cramped cabin, which strangely was almost starting to feel like home.

She knew what was there for breakfast – Cai had brought bacon and bread at the harbour, and there were tea and milk and eggs in the larder. If someone had asked her to translate one of Horace's Odes from Old Latin, or about the African Wars of five hundred years ago, or to state the achievements of the Emperor Gaius Maximus, she could have done that, no problem. But cook bacon and eggs for three working men? Hmm.

Luckily, rescuing Don from his hangovers had given her a little kitchen-sense. She put a match to the little oil burner and put the kettle on to boil. Then she fished out a greasy frying pan and peeled off rashers of bacon from the thick pile. This was like no bacon she'd ever seen before, yellow fat, saturated with salt, barely streaked with lean. She lit the second burner. Almost at once, the bacon started to frizzle and jump, startling her. It took her some time to work out how to turn the burner down to the right heat, but she managed, and soon it was cooking away less violently.

She didn't know how to make toast on the burners, so she hacked the bread into thick slices and fried them in

80

the swimming fat. They seemed to crisp and brown all right, and she managed not to burn them. Then the kettle started to boil, and she had to rush around finding the tea things. Finally, with the bacon and fried bread stacked on a plate, she realised she hadn't cooked the eggs. She didn't trust herself to fry them, but she'd watched Catti scrambling eggs – one of the few things her mother would eat when she was feeling fragile. So Livvy broke eggs into a bowl, whisked them up hurriedly with a fork and poured them into the still greasy pan, where they soon congealed into a kind of yellow lump. Ugh. Well, she had no intention of eating any of this. But she'd successfully cooked breakfast – she felt foolishly pleased with herself.

She wiped a greasy hand across her sweaty forehead, and let out a sigh. Then she turned to see Cai standing in the doorway of the cabin, a sly smile on his face.

'How long have you been standing there?' she said crossly.

The smile broke into a grin. 'Come on, I'll help you serve up.'

He slapped the greasy food onto plates, while she poured tea – lots of sugar, like she used to do for Don. Then she saw that he'd laid out four plates. She imagined all that grease churning through her system and coming out through the pores of her skin – ugh – it would kill her!

'I'm not eating this,' she said, when he'd come back to the hold after taking the men their food.

'Suit yourself,' he said shortly, and taking his own plate, started to eat rapidly. 'Hmm. These eggs are a bit solid. You could plaster cracks in the wall with them.'

'Well, I've never cooked them before,' she replied indignantly. Then she realised that actually she was quite hungry after all. She decided to try just a forkful of egg. Nothing like as good as Catti's; she'd have to try harder next time. And whatever did fried bread taste like? Cai was scoffing his greedily. She tried a bite. Before she knew it, she'd eaten the whole unhealthy plateful. Well. Tomorrow she'd try to live on just fruit, if she could get some.

She hoped for some kind of compliment from Cai, but all he said was, 'I've got to go back on deck now. Those plates won't wash themselves up, by the way.'

So she had to put on another kettle, and then try to wash the stack of greasy plates, with only soda to soften the hot water. She'd seen Catti scrub and stack plates before, but had never realised how you felt your hands were being scoured raw as well. Everything was a lesson, she thought.

Later that morning, they arrived at Verulam. There was a tannery near the dock area, which sent out blasts of foul air. Cai's father and uncle were off to the races for a couple of hours.

'Don't you want to go?' Livvy asked Cai as the two men set off.

He shook his head. 'I'm not about to watch that pair gamble away my ma's housekeeping. But we can't stay here – it stinks. Come on, let's go for a walk.'

Once they'd got past the docks and the tanneries, Verulam seemed to be a sleepy little town, of small brick houses set in walled gardens. There was almost no-one around, apart from some children playing and a milkman's cart. They found a little park, almost deserted in the winter chill, apart from a shivering mother disconsolately pushing her children on the swings. Cai and Livvy sat down on a bench among a litter of empty beer bottles and chip papers. 'Looks like this is someone's favourite spot,' she said with a grimace, shoving the litter away with her foot.

'Fussy,' he said.

Fussy! She who cooked fry-ups, and slept in a cabin with three men!

'What are you smiling at?' he asked, giving her a sideways look.

But she wasn't going to tell him that. So she changed the subject. 'You're dead good at that guitar,' she said. 'Who taught you?'

He blinked in surprise. 'No-one taught me. I taught myself.'

'Oh.' She guiltily remembered Mrs Rees and those expensive lessons. 'I play – I *played* – the violin. The guitar seems more fun, though. And you are good. I'm not just saying that.'

Cai seemed to be suppressing a smile of pleasure and fell silent for a few moments as though he wasn't used to compliments. Then he said, 'I'd like to play properly. Go round the pubs. Make a living.'

'Why don't you?'

'Because we've only got waterway licences, remember? All my dad's lot have been on the canals for years. Dad used to sing, you'd be surprised to know. Had a good voice, too, once. But no chance of using it, except on the way back from the pub.'

'What a waste.'

'I stayed with my ma's family once. In the west. No permits there. Sometimes I think I'd like to just take off and head in that direction.'

'Max had family in the west too,' she said. 'He really liked it there.' The atmosphere suddenly stiffened and

83

she regretted mentioning Max's name. Inadvertently, she'd managed to turn a conversation about Cai into one about herself.

'This Max . . .' he said, after a little while. 'Was he like . . . your boyfriend?'

'No. We were just like brother and sister really. What?' For Cai had given a disbelieving snort.

'That brother-and-sister business,' he said. 'Heard it before. Lasts about five minutes usually.'

'Well, in our case it was true,' she said indignantly. 'I'd known him forever. I couldn't think of him . . . like that. Really.'

'I believe you,' he said.

Why did he care? Surely it couldn't be . . . But he'd given no sign at all of being interested in her as anything more than a curiosity, a posh girl in disguise, just seeing how long she could keep up the pretence. They had nothing in common, really. People were always telling her how you couldn't cross the barrier of class. A pleb would always be a pleb, they said, no matter what. There was a nasty proverb about dressing a pig in satin. Centuries of refinement, they said, of superior breeding, of Roman blood, had given patricians an edge when it came to civilised behaviour and intelligence.

But what if they were wrong, all those superior people? What if a pleb and a patrician were just the same under the skin? She'd met some high-class boys with good connections who were nothing but braying oafs. What if a pleb could also be thoughtful and sensitive, someone you could have a long conversation with, talking about things you didn't think you could talk about with anybody, who you didn't want to say goodbye to? What if a pleb was someone you *fancied?*

# 11

That evening, back on board the boat, she felt confident enough to offer to cook the meal. It was macaroni, and she made the mistake of putting it in a pan of cold water and bringing it to the boil, so that eventually it was overcooked and looked like a mound of white maggots. Added to which, she had no idea how to turn it into macaroni cheese – Catti seemed to make some kind of sauce, she recalled. Thinking of Catti's cooking reminded her of her mother – where was she now? Where had they sent her, and why hadn't she written to Ishtar? She was vulnerable and drug-dependent – whatever had happened to her, it didn't feel good. Livvy wasn't close to her mother, but it didn't stop her worrying, and wondering.

Still, she had a task to do, and there was nothing else but to get on with it. So she chopped cheese and stirred it in lavishly with loads of butter. All Cai said, when he saw the steaming dish was, 'Hmm. Reckon you've got half a week's butter ration in there, miss.' But when the men staggered down – after the races they'd spent a couple of hours in the pub – it didn't seem that they'd notice any refinements of cuisine, and they shovelled it down without a word. Cai grinned at her – she had no idea whether she was passing all the tests he was setting her – but after they'd eaten, they went up on deck. The smell from the tannery had died down a little, and two or three other little boats were moored there, with cooking smells wafting from them, beneath a coldly glittering winter sky.

'Smells better than my macaroni cheese did,' she said, sniffing the air.

'Your macaroni cheese was all right,' he said.

'Still, I'm learning, I guess.'

'You certainly are.'

They leaned on the rail together, looking out at the canal. Sometimes a man on the neighbouring boat called out, and Cai replied. Another little boat chugged in, and found a mooring amid a great deal of noise and shouting. Cai and Livvy stood together in companionable silence. At one point, he turned to her, and she thought – or did she imagine it – that he seemed about to put an arm around her. But then the boat sounded its hooter loudly, like a warning to stop, and instead, he said, 'We ought to get back in, I guess. It's getting cold out here.'

Another night spent in her cramped corner. Once again, she didn't imagine she was going to sleep, and once again, she slept, heavily and throughout the night. When she woke up, she felt surprisingly fresh, even though she hadn't had a proper wash for days; her eyes were sticky and her hair tousled (thank goodness it was short). And yet, the cabin seemed a comfortable and familiar place, as though she'd known it all her life.

She was cold, she ached, she was embarrassed at using the toilet and she was scared. The men teased and she hated that. Every time she thought of Max it was like a wound opening up. And her mother was an anxiety too, and even Tony . . .

She was more alone than she'd ever been; she couldn't rely on a soul. And she was heading into the unknown, and she wasn't sure that she'd measure up.

But also, she never wanted this strange journey to end – she could not remember feeling so free and happy.

And in an odd way, the very uncertainty, the unpredictability of her life now, was exhilarating. She

86

felt fired-up and energised. In Ishtar College, she remembered, she'd always been tired and lethargic. Everything was an effort; her limbs felt heavy and reluctant. Now, although she was confined to this cramped boat, she felt light as air. If only she really were Glyn Howells, and could spend her days going up and down this quiet waterway, with Cai!

London opening out before her suddenly, as the canal entered the wide curve of the Thames, made her feel breathless: the stench of sewage and fish, the cacophony of noise as great ships edged into the narrow spaces of the port, and voices yelled in a variety of languages. Lights shone and dazzled, their reflections jostling in the oily water, crimson and silver and green; cargoes rumbled and rolled their way down causeways into crowded warehouses; on ground slicked with mud and oil and tar.

That morning, in a quiet moment, she and Cai had pored over maps of London. Cousin Lena lived in an eastern suburb, and Cai believed there was a nearby tram route. She'd traced her way through the pattern of roads. A canal passed close by and Don had told her that the house was the last one by the common – a patch of green showed this on the map. Livvy had a good memory and the plan fixed itself in her mind. She hoped she could find the right house once she'd got off the tram at the Lea Stadium. Anyway, Cai had promised he'd go with her – the *Diligence* was due to spend a couple of days in the city. All her nervousness rose up again – another strange place, more strange people. But maybe with Cai to show her the way, it would seem just a little more bearable.

This London was nothing like the elegant place she'd visited before. Cai took her through the very oldest district, the city around the docks, still surrounded in part by its ancient crumbling wall. There were dark, sooty little streets of high windowless buildings, and gloomy factories with smoke-belching chimneys, factories processing fish-sauce, or glue, or sugar, or beer. A heavy cloud of smoke hung over everything, and she could feel the grit in her lungs.

Tucked between factories and warehouses, however, were ruined temples, a crumble of fallen columns and porticos sprouting fireweed and purple buddleia, the once creamy stone soot-blackened, to remind them that this sad decaying area had been the heart of the city.

'I'm going to show you something,' said Cai. 'Just round the next corner. Better stay close to the wall, though.'

They hurried through the narrow dark streets of dockland, just the occasional pub or café open, and then into wider streets of dingy offices and warehouses. This was the London of the Caesars, essentially the London of two thousand years ago. Fashionable London had moved west and north, and everything here had seen better days.

He led her up a narrow street, along slimy cobbles. The street opened out suddenly into a square paved all over with flat, pale stones. The square was dominated by a building complex, behind high iron railings and iron gates. A courtyard led to a low narrow building, rising in the centre to a portico of tall classical columns. Unlike the old ruins, the stone was golden and clean, the carving crisp. But there was something bleak and inhuman about the place, with its rows of ordered windows, the tall, out-of-scale columns, some proportion that wasn't quite right, some human dimension missing. A group of men in military uniform was standing in the courtyard, chatting and laughing. A big sign, green and gold, hung by the gate; an image of a sun with feathery rays erupting from it – the symbol of Sol Invicta, the Unconquered Sun. Livvy felt a sudden cold shiver. 'But it's so huge!' she said, recalling the little Mithras temples dotted about Wroxeter.

'This building's fairly new, I think,' said Cai. 'But there's been a temple here forever. You can go round some of it, apparently. They try and recruit you for the army. A mate of mine did it once and said he nearly got sucked in. But you don't get to see anything. All the secret stuff goes on round the back, I reckon.'

'Have you ever been in?'

Cai shook his head. 'Spooks me, all that nonsense. But you could. At least Glyn could. Strictly no women, of course.'

'No thanks,' said Livvy. 'But I'd love to know just what goes on.'

'So would the Governor, I bet,' said Cai.

The soldiers stopped talking and one of them cast a routine glance in the direction of Livvy and Cai, practised eyes just checking out any strangers on their periphery. She recognised their colours – they were Silurians and Iberians. And another uniform with a green cockade that she didn't recognise. Instinctively, Cai and Livvy shrunk out of sight, turned the corner and began to run. They ran down several dark streets, Cai steering her from time to time.

At last they came out beneath the old city walls. Though they were much tumbled down and buildings had been rammed against them, you could make out their contours in many places and they still enclosed the older part of the city.

But now things suddenly opened out into lights and noise. There was a huge square, so big you could hardly see the far sides, where steam trams whined and gasped, their shining steel tracks making apparently random patterns in the cobbles. There were lit buildings all round the square, night cafés and seedy hotels. Military Police were stopping people at random, checking their papers, and Livvy noticed with a shudder that they had guns. Even though it wasn't a curfew night, they were keeping a close watch. Livvy and Cai decided that it would be safer to walk than to take the tram. By ducking and diving around the square, through doorways and up and down alleys, they managed to avoid the MPs and at last found themselves on Cambridge Road.

The road was wide and bleak; it charged through straggling suburbs, pubs, cheap cafés, garment factories and blacksmiths. Stadiums and scruffy bathhouses loomed, empty and ghostly in the evening light.

After about two miles, Cai took a right fork through a scrubby wood that turned soon into a marshy plain. 'We're near the canal here,' he said. 'Now we'll have to ask around a bit.'

They did, choosing people who didn't look as if they'd report them to the police. They asked a dim-looking woman with three screaming kids, a half-dazed road sweeper and a doddery old lady with a small dog. At last they found an unmade road, meandering through trees and overgrown bushes. The gathering twilight made everything hard to discern; if they didn't find the house soon, they'd be in trouble.

The last house in the road was an eccentric cottage, all fancy gables and twisted chimneys. But it had seen better days; the garden was so overgrown with thick evergreens that very little light could have penetrated, the paintwork was chipped and faded and one or two of the windows had been boarded up. Well, even Don had said his cousin was peculiar.

'Oh dear,' said Livvy, looking at it uneasily.

'Want me to come in with you?'

'Better not.'

'I'll wait here for a bit, just see you inside. Then I'll be off.'

She'd been so taken up with getting here that she hadn't realised how close they were to parting. Now suddenly it dawned on her. 'Will I see you again?' she asked awkwardly.

'Did you want to?' he said, equally awkward. She nodded.

'Well, I guess we're in this together anyway,' he said. 'Look, we go back up again tomorrow. But at the end of the week we'll be in London again. I'll come over here and find you, shall I?'

She nodded. She didn't know what to do next, but he leaned across and gave her a quick kiss on the cheek. 'In you go, Liv. Good luck.'

The front door was so faded that it was hard to tell what colour it had been once – maybe blue, maybe green. A thick mat of rustling leaves had blown onto the front step. When Livvy rang the bell, it echoed in the depths of the house, and set up a cacophony of barking dogs. But for a long time nothing happened. Half-relieved, she was just going to go back and find Cai when the door opened and an incredibly ancient tiny woman stood there.

'M – Miss Lena Macdonald?' stammered Livvy.

'What do you want?'

'I wanted to see Miss Lena. I've got a letter from . . .'

The ancient woman didn't wait to hear. She shut the door with a slam, and Livvy could hear footsteps clattering into the interior. Then the door opened again. 'She says you're to come in.'

Livvy followed her into a dark hallway. Her footsteps rang on old mosaic. The dogs still barked. Then the woman flung open a door. Livvy received a brief impression of clutter and smell, glimpsed a hatchet face staring at her across the room, then the dogs flung themselves at her.

There were two of them, little short-legged dogs barking wildly and not very amicably. Livvy guessed this was some sort of a test. She had never been very good with dogs – her mother hated them – but she decided to pretend she was. Ignoring the two human faces staring at her, she made a desperate play for the dog-approval vote. Being careful to stand perfectly still, she said, '*Good* boy! Lovely boy! Well done! *Aren't* you a lovely boy then?' She said this several times. After a while she held out a tentative hand. They still barked and yapped around her ankles, but one of them sniffed the hand, then retreated a little. So did the other. 'Good, good boy!' she said between gritted teeth. She thought she glimpsed the beginning of a tail-wag.

Only then did the hatchet face react. 'Argos! Diamond!' she growled in a voice like gravel. 'Here! *Now!*' Both dogs trotted meekly over and sat at her feet.

Livvy had passed the first test.

'So. What do you want, boy?'

The old lady who stared at her had a rumpled face like a squashed pug-dog. She could never have been pretty. Her skin was the colour of old string, and so was her hair. She wore a filthy jumper, a strange, long, tiered skirt and her feet were jammed into huge, fat carpet slippers.

Livvy swallowed. 'I'm not a boy. I'm Livia Marcel. And I've got a letter from your cousin.'

She fished in her trouser pocket and brought out the letter which by now was crumpled and dirty.

The old lady sniffed. She took the letter from Livvy, opened it and read it through. It took a long time. When she'd read it, she passed it to the other ancient woman to read. This took even longer. Livvy shifted from one foot to the other.

When – finally – the other old woman had folded the letter up and handed it back to her, Miss Lena said, 'He was always daft, that cousin of mine. So what's up with the other one? Is he a girl too?'

'What other one?' said Livvy, taken aback. She had no idea she'd been spotted.

'The boy you came with. *Is* he a boy?'

'He just came with me to help me find the way.'

'So why is he hanging about outside then?'

'Just making sure I'm all right.'

'Just making sure the dogs don't eat you. Or I don't. Or Sybil.' She gave a cackling laugh. Then she stopped. 'Well, go on, girl. Livia Marcel, whatever your name is really. Bring him in. I can't have boys lurking.'

# 12

But Cai had already vanished when she went outside to look for him. She was glad of that – she didn't want to bring him in here with these two witchy old ladies. And once again, she had to repeat her story. They both listened, from time to time twitching or sniffing, but neither interrupted. She saw a strange avid gleam in their eyes, and it occurred to her that her story was probably the most exciting thing that had happened to them in years.

But she knew she wasn't going to get any sympathy at the end of it. Miss Macdonald merely sniffed and said, 'Well, you are in a mess, aren't you? Suppose we don't want you?'

'Then I'll have to hide out somewhere else.'

'Where?' said the old woman. And she gave a cackle. 'You haven't got anywhere else, have you?' While Livvy was digesting this, she went on, 'All right. You can stay here for a bit. Sybil and I are too old to worry about the army coming to get us. They don't torture people our age. But don't get the wrong idea; we aren't cosy old ladies, you know.'

'I didn't think you were,' said Livvy.

Miss Macdonald cackled again. Sybil simply stared impassively. 'And you'll have to work for your keep, you know. My garden needs clearing. Are you capable of clearing a garden?'

'I used to help my father,' said Livvy. Saying it made her remember it. She went quiet for a moment and the sadness must have shown in her eyes, for Miss Macdonald peered at her suddenly and said, 'Who do you think killed your father then?'

Livvy sat up, in real shock. 'Nobody killed my father!' she exclaimed. 'It was an accident.'

'Oh yes?'

'Yes! A steam car he was travelling in blew up. The driver was killed too. And another soldier.'

'So? They killed three men to get one. It's not unknown, you know.'

'But . . .' said Livvy, suddenly feeling helpless. 'They wouldn't kill him. He was a hero. He had a medal.'

'Heroes aren't to everyone's taste.'

'Yes,' said Livvy, floundering. 'But he wasn't. I mean . . . why do you think so?'

'Why?' said the old lady sharply. 'Because it makes too many dead people, doesn't it, to be accidental. Your friend what's his name, and the servant girl, and they're out to get you too.'

'Yes, but . . .' said Livvy stubbornly. She realised that what the old lady was telling her she had always known in her heart, though her head had been in denial. And now that it was there, the realisation could never be dislodged.

Once again, thought Livvy, as she hacked away at an especially nasty thorn bush, all the pieces of her life had been chucked up in the air, to land in an apparently random and meaningless pattern. She'd now passed two nights in Miss Macdonald's airless and damp spare bedroom, and was halfway through the second day of hacking down the jungly garden that surrounded the house, the price she'd had to pay for hospitality. In the newspapers, the headlines still appeared:

**FEARS GROW FOR MISSING GIRL**.

She just hoped her mother was in no state to see them.

It was good of Miss Lena, of course it was, to be looking after her. Sheltering somebody whom the Military Police were looking for was no mean matter.

But, thought Livvy, they could have been just a little nicer about it. The thorn bush ripped her arm in an especially vicious manner just to remind her that she wasn't here to enjoy herself.

Underneath this jungle, she was beginning to realise, a pretty garden lay hidden. She'd already uncovered a stone bench, and pulled festoons of ivy from an arch over the path. And strangely, the more she worked, the calmer she began to feel. It was as though, with all the exercise, something in her brain was taking over the problem for her and quietly working on the solution.

Because there *was* a solution; she was starting to feel sure of that. There were things she could do to make things better for herself. It was just a matter of finding out what they were.

For some reason her mind kept returning to her father. He loved working in the garden, and when he had spare time, which wasn't very often, he worked there, and she always helped him. He would talk to her, almost as though she were an adult, about anything and everything, explaining things to her, describing all the strange things he'd seen on his campaigns. She would rush around, desperate to be helpful, hacking ivy off the walls, scraping moss from the paths, or cleaning the green scum from the fountain. In one of the wall alcoves, there stood a real antique, an ancient statue from the days of the Caesars, a head of Minerva, worn and smoothened, until you could hardly see her face. But he'd loved that statue. She remembered him saying to her once, 'You see, old Minerva knows all the secrets of the world. If you want to know something, just ask her. She'll tell you.' Which was strange, because he wasn't a man to be sentimental about the gods.

Livvy sighed, and returned to her garden tasks, much less fascinating in this fatherless world. She was hot and sticky; a waft of her own perspiration rose up to her – ugh. Glyn Howells must get some new clothes soon, or no-one would want to be near him.

'You don't want to go that way, mate,' said a voice at her ear. Livvy turned to see a large young man, lounging in a doorway, with a day's growth of beard on his chin and wearing a gold earring. His eyes were narrowed. They were alone in the alleyway she'd been so unwise as to follow. For a moment she panicked, but then she realised that she wasn't a girl being chatted up by a possibly dangerous lout; she was just another boy.

'What's wrong with that way?' she said, trying not to squeak in a girlish way.

But unlike Cai, he seemed quite taken in by her disguise, Maybe she was becoming more convincing.

'What's wrong, mate?' he echoed. 'Well, nothing if you like having your papers checked. There's a roadblock. The Scum out in force.'

'Oh. Thanks,' she said. 'I wanted to get to the flea-market. Is there another way?'

'Back the way you came, up past the stadium, then first right. That way you'll avoid them. They're all over the place at the moment.'

'Why?' she said. 'Has something happened?'

'Dunno, mate. But they say the Emperor's going to die, any minute.'

'Yeah, I heard that too,' she said, trying to spark off a bit of gossip. 'Wonder what'll happen then?'

'Your guess as good as mine, mate. Won't be good, that's all I know. More taxes, less money. More bloody Scum all over the place.'

'Yeah,' Livvy agreed, trying to sound like Cai. 'Too right. Anyway, cheers, mate. I'll try and find that market.'

She went off feeling quite pleased with herself.

The market was cheap and crowded. Stalls were heaped with secondhand and cheap new clothes. She bought Glyn Howells another pair of woollen trousers, grey, and a flecked wool sweater that she hoped was baggy enough to hide her figure. (She'd always resented her small breasts – but now, under a tight vest and a baggy sweater, they weren't going to give her away.) She bought woollen socks, and realised with a shock that what she really needed was underwear, and unless she was to draw attention to herself, she'd have to buy blokes' pants. It was a bad moment. However, she did find a couple of pairs that could have done for either sex, and paid for them quickly before anyone noticed. Everyone else sorting through the piles of clothes was female. She felt uncomfortable, and got out as quickly as she could.

Still, she'd got new clothes and avoided a police check. That counted as a success, of sorts.

So she was feeling quite pleased with herself as she left the market, crossed a road, and took a short cut across the centre of a run-down square, where leaves blew into an empty fountain, and dossers lounged on benches. Probably she'd just let her guard slip. For suddenly she was aware of a kind of darkness in her peripheral vision. Before she could move, the darkness had edged in, and she was being gripped hard, both arms, by two people at her sides, and a voice was hissing in her ear, 'You come with us; you don't make a sound, right? There's a knife, so no clever business.'

# 13

*'Don't look at us,'* one hissed. There was a man and a girl. The man wore grey woollen trousers and heavy boots; the girl had a plaid skirt and fabric shoes. Poor people's garments. The man could have passed for Roman but the girl had a strong Cymric accent. *'Don't scream!'*

They had manoeuvred her to an empty bench. Behind her, the road rumbled away beyond a thick privet hedge; in front, the square stretched empty, apart from the indifferent dossers. She felt the sharp jab of the knife at her ribs. From a distance, they must have looked like a group of friends, the man who now had his arm around her waist, the girl cuddling close.

Livvy found her voice. 'Who are you? What do you want?'

'We want what you've got,' said the girl.

'I haven't got anything.'

'We think you have.'

'Tell me who you are.'

'We're on your side, actually,' said the man. 'You co-operate. You'll see.'

'Are you *Bleiddiaid*?'

'Call us what you like. A name is only a name.'

'So what do you want?'

'Now, those others – they want you dead. We want

99

you alive. *Don't look at us.'* This last said with a sudden hiss and a jab of the knife as she wriggled in their grasp.

Livvy winced. 'Look. Tell me what you think I've got and I'll tell you if I've got it.' Not very logical but the best she could manage at the moment.

'*They* think you have something that will lead you to us.'

'Theta?'

'So you've heard of them?'

'Nothing really. Only the name. But that girl at Ishtar . . . Bronwen. And Max, my friend Max . . . they said . . . And now they're dead.'

'Yes,' said the man. 'Poor Nia. That was Bronwen's real name. A good little operative. It was because of you she died, you know.'

'*Because* of me?' Another unpleasant fact to be faced up to, and one which again, she realised she'd known about in her heart.

'She didn't have to help you. But your friend, Gwydion, he was anxious to make sure you were safe. And he'd been helping us, sort of. This was something in return.'

'How had he been helping you?'

'Bits of this and that from the barracks. Nothing world-shattering, but everything's useful.'

So that was why Max had been so keen to hang around the Spread Eagle. And no wonder, given his usual lack of subtlety, someone had got suspicious about him . . .

'Is that why they're after me too? Because of what Max – *Gwydion* – was saying?'

The man didn't answer. 'Champagne revolutionary, we call his sort. All enthusiasm, and no practical sense.'

Livvy was outraged. 'How dare you . . .'

But she was silenced by another jab of the knife. 'What's done is done, Livia Marcel. Now we move on.'

'So how did you find me?'

'Who do you think forged your papers? We know what goes on. The *Diligence,* wasn't it? Tracked you to that witch's house. But *they* don't know. Yet.'

'Somebody said my father was murdered,' Livvy said. 'And Max's father. Was that your lot did that?'

'Not us, Livia. Why should we? Your father was no threat to us. But he was murdered, no doubt of that.'

'So why was he murdered?'

'We're going round in circles here. Because of what he knew. And we have evidence that what he knew, you know.'

'You're wrong. I'm sorry. I'm not really sure I'd have told you, even if I did know something. But I *don't* know anything. I swear . . . on the tombs of my ancestors.'

'Oh yes?' laughed the girl. 'Swear on something else if you want us to believe you.'

Livvy was getting angry now. 'I'll swear on whatever you want. I-don't-know-*anything*.'

'All right,' said the man. ' Maybe you really don't think you do. But somewhere or other you do. Let's pool our resources. Let's be friends. See what we come up with.'

'Take that blasted knife away if you want us to be friends.'

'No chance of that yet, I'm afraid, Livia Marcel. But tell you what. I'll talk to you. See what you make of it.'

'All right.' Did she have a choice?

'Theta. I see you've heard of them. Not many people have, so that's something that suggests we're right about you. Mithraian initiates, of a special secret sort, secret even to other initiates. At a level that the common soldiers can aspire to, who's to say how many? Thousands and thousands, maybe, spread throughout the Empire, and increasing fast. Common aims and lots of secrecy. Small cells, each independent, knowing nothing about the other cells. That way, even if someone defects, knowledge can't spread too far. But then – and now we're getting to the nitty-gritty – in charge of all this nonsense – just one group of men. Eight, we think. It's Theta's significant number after all. Just eight men. Known only to each other, known by code name to everyone else. Now, who are they? That's what we need to know right now.'

'So what's it all *for?*' asked Livvy, interested in spite of herself. 'Why do they need all this?'

'Good question. Let's look at this moment in history. Emperor Julian. Longest serving Emperor in the history of your bloodstained Empire. And, in spite of what they tell you in your nice little schools, not much cop as ruler, either. Corrupt and lazy and steered by advisors, for year after year after year.'

'And now he's dying,' Livvy said. She began to see which way this story was tending.

'Exactly. Who's his heir? That useless grandson of his probably. The Emperor has probably chosen him, and the Senate will probably ratify his choice, just as it always has. But this time . . .'

'Theta's got different plans?'

'They said you were a bright girl. Theta, using Britain as a power base, plans to change all that. The Governor – well, they'll assassinate him, probably.'

'Roman soldiers assassinate a Roman Governor? Never,' said Livvy stubbornly.

'You people believe all the old clichés, don't you? Assassinate the Governor, and their well-oiled system

102

slips smoothly into place. Give or take a small civil war, but who's counting?'

'And what is this . . . system?'

'Oh, you'll love it. A return to the bad old days, and then some. Military rule, even more total than we have now. Return of the old punishments, scourgings, crucifixion, gladiatorial combat, you name it. All propped up, of course, by slavery.'

'*Slavery?*' gasped Livia. 'They couldn't. They wouldn't.'

'Oh, they will. Mop up all your enemies that way, just like Julius Caesar did. All resistance put down, all rebels enslaved. And a cheap and easy labour force. Send the prices down and the standard of living up. Like what you hear so far?'

'Tell her about their plans for women,' said the girl.

'Oh yes. If you ever had any thoughts of getting the vote, which I believe some of you are campaigning for, forget it. Women to become the property of their husbands or fathers. Single women and widows to be forcibly married off, or cast off into prostitution, who cares? Your husband or father can legally kill you, beat you, whatever. Not a crime. Oh, and no vote for most of the plebs, either, of course. Only one-up from slavery. No religious freedom, naturally; any stray Jews, Christians, Isisians or Belonians, they'll be gone too. Just the one state religion, and death to anyone who doesn't believe. Like what you're hearing so far?'

'But how can you be so sure of this? If it's so secret?'

'Oh, we get everywhere. We've even infiltrated Theta, though the fate of those guys, if they're ever found out, is unimaginable. They have cyanide capsules, of course, in case it comes to that. Brave men. Brave beyond brave.'

'Tell her about that school of hers,' said the girl.

Livvy had become tired of her gloating promptings. '*You* tell me. We're talking about Ishtar, I presume?'

'So what do you think they trained all those girls up for?'

'Well, I thought marriage to old officers,' said Livvy wearily. 'You, no doubt, are going to tell me differently.'

'Well, some of them really do get married off. Lots of palaver and fanfares, and then stuck out in some foreign dump forever. But the others – well, it's high class prostitution, really.'

'They wouldn't do that,' snapped Livvy, remembering all those innocent, enthusiastic girls. 'Someone would find out.'

'Didn't you notice how many of them were orphans? Nobody to find out. A constant supply of well-educated, submissive virgins.'

'I don't believe you.'

The man broke in again. 'What happens to old Ishtarians is no-one's concern except their own. We've more important things to think of. Now, Livia Marcel, if your father didn't share his information with you, whatever it was, why do they think differently? Maybe you have access to something without knowing.'

'I really can't think.'

'Your father's papers. What happened to them?'

'They cleared out his office in the barracks. Mi . . .' She broke off suddenly.

She could sense them both turning to look at her. 'Your what?' said the man sharply.

Livvy recollected herself fast. 'My . . . my father's friend . . . Uncle . . . Commander Flavian came down

104

too. What was left, Tony, my brother took away. I've never seen any of that stuff.' She swallowed in relief. They seemed not to have noticed her quick footwork.

'Well, what about valuable items in your house? Was there a safe?'

'Yes, but there was nothing there. I was there when Tony opened that. Just some share certificates, some medals and some of my grandmother's jewellery. No secrets.'

'Do you know what your father was working on before he died?'

She shook her head. 'No. But he seemed tired. And anxious. I noticed that. I thought he was cross with me.'

'And Madoc's father? Can you tell us anything more about him?'

'No. Except that Max never believed it was suicide. He said his dad had promised to take him to the circus that weekend, because it was Max's birthday. He said his father wouldn't have broken a promise, even if he was depressed, which Max said he wasn't anyway.'

'Did you believe he committed suicide?'

'I don't know. You believe what you're told, don't you? It was three years ago. Tony told me Max's father was unstable. I couldn't see any reason not to believe that.'

'And your father never dropped a hint? Think.'

'Look,' said Livvy. 'Three years ago I was twelve. Do you think that if my father had this . . . this dangerous knowledge that you're on about, he'd only tell one person, a twelve-year-old girl?'

'You're right,' said the man. 'It doesn't make much sense. But nonetheless, we think he did.'

'Anyway,' said Livia. 'Why does it matter to you? I thought your lot wanted the Empire to collapse.'

'Maybe we do, Livia. But not this way. Plus there've been some secret political negotiations which I can't tell you about. Greater powers for the Cymric Council, more independence, we hope. But not under this lot. Even we don't want a bloodbath. Well, it seems we're going round in circles. You have a think, and see if you come up with something. We'll stay in touch. Now listen. You stand up, and walk forward. Go out of the square. Don't even think of looking back.'

'I don't care who you are. I don't want to see your faces,' said Livia. 'I just want to go.'

'Then go. Just remember, don't look round.'


# 14


Livvy sat on the top deck of the West End steam tram, looking through misted-up windows. Mi . . . She'd been going to say Milo Faber, her father's adjutant, who'd been with him for years, though all of his campaigns. If anyone knew anything, Milo would. Only she wasn't about to serve him up to the *Bleiddiaid*. She wasn't sure how far she could trust those people; she had some sympathy with them, and the more she learned, the more sympathies she had; but some of the things they'd done, or were supposed to have done . . .!

She'd forgotten Milo, because she'd forgotten so much in the confusion of her father's death. He'd retired very suddenly after that, gone to live with his wife in one of the colonies favoured by ex-army men, somewhere in the west of London. She'd written to him, sending formal greetings on a couple of occasions and the address had stuck in her mind. 32 Aspen Drive,

Cordova Estate (most of these retirement estates were named after the warm places where many military families originated). Milo's family had been Iberian some generations ago, though Milo himself could not have been more British. It was odd – it had struck even her mother – the way Milo had wanted to break contact with the family of his beloved commander. Almost as if, Livvy now thought, he'd been frightened of keeping in touch.

So why? That was how, armed with a set of instructions squeezed out of the still grumpy Sybil, she found herself making the long journey across London, to see if she could add yet one more piece to this confusing and frightening jigsaw. The journey involved three trams each way: she'd taken the Cambridge Road tram to the old city walls at Norgate Place, and now she took the *Invicta* – the West End tram – which she would have to change at Muscovy Square, in the smart centre of the city.

In spite of the danger, part of her found the journey exhilarating, peering through the misty window at the winter shops, laden with goods for the Solstice, which would take place in a few days' time, eager shoppers wrapped in furs and shawls and carrying brightly-wrapped parcels. In the murk, colours gleamed with an electric magic, a crimson roll of fabric in a shop window, an array of blue perfume bottles. When she'd been to the city before, she'd travelled most of the time in closed carriages, only catching glimpses of the world outside. Now, in spite of everything, it was hers.

But the *Bleiddiaid* had shadowed her to Lena's house, and quite possibly were shadowing her now. She had no intention of leading them to Milo Faber. As for the others – the mysterious others who were after her blood – well, she hoped they were still looking for a lost Ishtar schoolgirl. Not for long, perhaps, but for the moment she was probably safe from them.

With a gasp of steam and a rattle of iron wheels, the tram clanged to a halt. 'Muscovy Square!' shouted the conductor. 'All change!' Livvy and everybody else scrambled off, and dispersed into the busy street.

Out in the smoky cold, Livvy looked around her. Muscovy Square – named after a long ago battle. Even at this time of year, thronged with tourists, feeding the pigeons, setting up camera tripods. Before her, the great gold-plated statue of Victory – the iconic image of modern London – spread huge wings. And on either side, the smart boulevards stretched away, to the Governor's Palace in one direction, to the Senate, to the London Temple, the Julian Basilica in the other.

Livvy had to catch the suburban tram – the *Palatine,* this one was pompously called – from a stop across the square. But she was not going to catch it straight away. She wanted to deceive anyone who might be following her. After all, no-one except herself and the mad old ladies knew where she intended to go. Let them think she was just enjoying the city and the Solstice crowds.

So she plonked herself down on a bench, and pretended to be watching pigeons like everyone else. Tourists gasped and pointed, studied their guide books. Children ran, gleefully scattering flocks of birds, and lovers giggled as they ducked beneath swooping wings.

Then, after twenty minutes – she had quite enjoyed all this, to be honest – she retraced her steps, and joined a queue of people waiting for the return *Invicta* to Norgate Place.

The tram rumbled up before her, and she clambered on, paying the conductor. 'Just one stop,' she whispered. She stood by the exit doors, hanging onto a swaying strap. At the next stop, she waited while the doors clanged open. Another horde of people climbed on – and as they did so, Livvy pushed her way off the tram through the crowd. She hoped that anybody following her would have lost her.

She was now in an unfamiliar street – but not so far from where she wanted to be. She took her bearings, and set off in a northerly direction, cutting through narrow streets of small coffee houses and newsagents. Soon, by this diversion, she had found her way to the north side of Muscovy Square. She noted the bus stop, and then dived into a shady doorway nearby, so she could wait more discreetly.

Finally, the suburban tram arrived, and she got on. A few people got on with her: a schoolboy, a woman with a baby, an old woman with a fur wrap, and an anxious-looking African. None looked like a Cymric terrorist.

Some forty minutes later, she had reached her stop. Sybil had told her what to ask for – the West London Arena – and there she disembarked. No dazzling colours here, just tired women laden with string bags of vegetables, or men hunched outside the betting kiosks, chilled in the misty late afternoon air. Cordova Estate was not far from here, Sybil said. Livvy asked a couple of people – as usual choosing the scruffiest and least prepossessing. Then, diving across the wide road, narrowly avoiding a steam tram and a few carts, nearly slipping on a mound of horse dung and another pile of wet leaves – she found herself in a quiet side road, then another. Across a small park, she could see the estate –

row upon row of small red-brick buildings, with only the now bare trees to soften the raw geometry.

The estate must have stretched for a quarter of a mile: two main roads, of flats, cafés, newsagents and grocers, intersecting a network of streets, all named after trees – Oak, Elm, Birch, Holly. Her head spun – how many trees could there possibly be in the world? Chestnut, Lime, Sycamore. Each of the neat little single-storey houses had a neat, square garden, planted with care if not imagination – ex-soldiers didn't usually make great gardeners. Pots of late chrysanthemums, winter-flowering cherry, thorny roses clipped hard back. Smoke puffed from each chimney; some houses had lamps lit in their windows against the bleak afternoon. Here and there, the cheering of a football match on the radio drifted through. A big match it was – Chester, the Black-and-Whites, playing the London team, Temple, the All Blues. It followed her in an undulating loop of sound, from street to street. One man was repairing his wooden gate; another carried rubbish to a dustbin. A child played on a small bicycle. Otherwise, all was still as the grave. She noticed she was back in Oak Street. Round in circles – though there were no circles here, just straight lines. She went back to the man mending the fence and asked him the way to Aspen. He looked at her as though she was mad and directed her with a couple of waves. Down one street, a left turn, then first right. She'd been very close several times.

32. Even bleaker than most of the bungalows – a high privet hedge, a wooden gate firmly shut, the front yard paved all over. Swept clean, windows concealed behind thick net. She went up the path and knocked.

Eventually she heard footsteps. The door opened a

little, on a chain. A woman peeped out. Small, plump, frizzy dyed-brown hair. Livvy recognised Milo's wife, though she couldn't remember her first name.

'Yes?' No smile.

'Mrs Faber, please can I see Milo? It's important.'

'Who *are* you?'

'It's about Captain Marcel. Please. It's important.'

The woman's reaction was sudden and violent. 'No!' she said. 'Go away. We've nothing to say!' And the door slammed, while Livvy stood open-mouthed, not sure what to do next.

It was opened again a few minutes later. 'Yes?' said a voice. Not friendly, but not in a state of panic. Livvy saw a little man, wearing dressing gown and pyjamas, weather-beaten, bright dark eyes and big nose, darkish thinning hair brushed over his skull. Milo. But he didn't recognise her. Why should he?

'Milo,' she said in a rush. 'I'm not a boy. I'm Livia Marcel. We're in trouble. We need your help.'

His eyes widened. The surprise on his face was suppressed almost as instantly as it had come. Soldiers had years of training in cutting off their emotions sharply. He looked over his shoulder to where his wife must have been still hovering in the corridor. 'Sorry,' he said loudly. 'Can't help you, I'm afraid. You'll have to go.'

Livvy's mouth fell open in disappointment. The little man looked over his shoulder again. Then he hissed, 'Bathhouse, end of the road. Ten minutes. Coffee shop. You'll be safe enough there. See you.'

And before Livvy had even closed her mouth, the door had shut fast again.

# 15

The bathhouse stood on a corner – its frontage on the main road nearly windowless, its shadowed entrance round the side. She slipped under the dark red-brick arch of the entrance. On the floor were cheap mosaics with a pattern of waves and fish; around her, from steamy caverns came the sound of laughing and splashes and shouts, everything muffled with a strange hollow echo. Men shuffled about in towels, and she glimpsed naked bodies. Not a place for a young lady, but it must be safe, or Milo wouldn't have sent her here. On the right-hand side of the entrance there was a café, a half-circle of windows set high up and misted with steam. Men sat hunched around a radio relaying the football match. Their cries of triumph or disaster echoed the excited gabble of the commentary. The man behind the counter barely cast a glance in her direction as he plonked down a mug of tea in exchange for a handful of dinars.

She took it to a table as far away from the radio as she could, and sat there, cradling it in her cold fingers, waiting for Milo. It reminded her of waiting in the Black Dragon – only a couple of weeks ago, but it seemed an eternity.

She waited for about fifteen minutes. The All-Blues had scored a goal and missed another, then Milo came in, wrapped in overcoat and scarf. He looked strange in civvies, artificial somehow, like an actor in costume. He too bought a tea and came towards her with a hesitant little grin.

'Sorry about all that,' he said. 'The missus, you see. She's terrified.' He looked at Livvy across the table. 'I'm doing security work now. I'm on nights. Hope you excused the pyjamas. Only,' he said, 'I knew you'd come. Sooner or later. Not like this, maybe,' – he pointed at her clothes – 'but sooner or later, miss. I knew they'd make the connection, like.'

'But Milo,' she said. 'I don't understand what's going on. They're after me, and I don't know why.'

'Your mother,' he said, 'and Master Antony. Are they all right?'

'Yes. No. I'm not sure. They've put my mother somewhere, a hospital or a clinic. I don't know where. And Tony's been posted away. I don't know where he is either. They tried to send me to Ishtar, only I ran away.'

He blew out through his teeth. 'Sounds as though they've tried to bury all of you alive, if you'll pardon the expression. But that's better than it might have been.'

Under a roar of groans as someone missed yet another goal, she leaned forward and hissed, 'Milo, do you think my father was murdered?'

He was quiet for a long time. Then he said, 'I wasn't sure at the time. It might have happened as they said. Some of those old carriages are pretty lethal. But I was scared, I admit that. So was the missus. Our lad's in the Fourteenth. Our daughter's married to a subaltern. She's out in Cyprus now. We didn't want anything to happen to them. My wife insisted we got out. Nearly broke my heart to leave the Legion. But at least I'm alive. We're all alive. When I heard about Captain Madoc, I was sure it wasn't an accident.'

'But why? Why, why, why? Was my father working on something? Did he know something? This . . . this Theta business. Do you know about that?'

Milo shook his head. 'Your father . . .' he said slowly, 'he was always looking into things. Human rights, that

113

sort of thing. Even if the army didn't like it. It got him noticed, and noticed by the wrong people. I worried about that. There were these Mithras creeps. Didn't operate in the open – very crafty, they were. Unless you wanted to join. Then they sucked you in, good and proper. Someone approached me once. I think what they wanted was for me to spy on your father. Didn't say it in so many words of course, went all round the houses. But that's what they meant, I'm sure of it. Told them where they could stuff their creepy religion. Didn't ask me after that.'

'But what did you know? What could you have told them?'

'That's it, miss. Couldn't have told them anything, even if I'd wanted to. Except . . .'

'Except . . .?'

'Your father. And Captain Madoc. I heard them talking once. I was in the next room. I was with this bloke – forgotten his name now, but he worked in the mess. He had a query about an officers' party they were holding at the weekend. Captain Madoc and your father came into the next door room. I should have coughed, made a noise, let them know we were there, but they didn't see us.'

'What did they say?'

'Well . . . Captain Madoc had just asked a question I couldn't hear. And your father replied, *No, not yet. I just need to tie up some loose ends.* Then he laughed. *Mind, if they knew* . . . He didn't finish the sentence, like.

'Then Captain Madoc . . . I remember this conversation like it was yesterday, miss, I've gone over it so many times . . . he said, *Felix, I'm not trying to be defeatist, but you're very vulnerable here. If anything happened to you, all this would go for nothing.* And your father, he said, still sort of laughing, but a bit afraid . . . *If anything happened to me, Livvy'd know just where to look . . .'*

A surge of cheering. Temple had scored another goal. The wave of raucous joy burst over the café. Livvy sat frozen.

Milo said, 'That's about it, miss. Captain Madoc said, *You haven't told her, have you?* And he said, your father, *What do you take me for? . . .*

'That was all. I scraped my chair, made a bit of a noise. They saw us, they coughed and changed the subject. But this other bloke, he'd heard it all too. And like I said, I didn't really know much about him. Could have talked to anyone, and I'm pretty sure he did. A week later, your father was dead.'

'But I don't know,' said Livia. 'I don't know what he could have meant . . .'

But then . . . she realised she did . . .

# 16

The journey back to Lena Macdonald's house was worse than she anticipated. For one thing, she was late – journeys across London took much longer than she expected – and every minute that passed brought her closer to curfew. 'You should be all right, miss, if you hurry,' Milo had said, which wasn't reassuring. The tram to Muscovy Square was late, with the result that she missed the five-o-clock *Invicta* and had to wait for the five-thirty. The happy festive mood she had noted

115

before had vanished. Instead, people huddled uneasily, stamping from foot to foot in the cold, looking over their shoulders. Groups of soldiers and Military Police seemed much in evidence, the glint of their uniforms showing suddenly in the twilight. In front of her, in the queue, a girl and her mother fretted. 'I'm sure it'll be fine, Ma,' said the girl. 'We'll be home in no time.'

'But what if we aren't?' moaned the mother. 'What can we do?'

'Ma, I told you, it'll be *fine,* OK? Now just stop fussing.'

But the girl seemed anxious too, and when the tram finally pulled up, everyone appeared relieved.

In the seat in front of her someone scanned the evening paper, and she turned away, in case there was another *Missing Girl* headline. But the reader flicked through the pages rapidly. The Emperor was dying. The world was about to be turned upside down, and even if people didn't have the dangerous corrosive knowledge she now possessed, they were worried.

For she did know, she was sure of it, just what her father had been talking about. She knew how to find out whatever it was that he'd been working on. And to test that would mean a journey back to Wroxeter, the most dangerous place in Britain for her at present.

Yet, if she didn't try, this situation might go on indefinitely; there would be no way out of being endlessly on the run, no end to the danger her mother faced, and Tony. She would have to find a way.

At Norgate Square, she scanned the big clock anxiously. If the tram came on time, if there was not much traffic on Cambridge Road, if she ran at the other end, she might just beat the curfew. There were few people about in the square now – they scuttled into passages and doorways with their heads down. A cold wind blew litter and dust along the pavements and into gutters. Offices and shops had already been boarded up.

But eventually, the tram came, and she went onto the top deck.

A man read the sporting papers, two women gossiped languidly, a young man looked bored and another older man leaned back as if to sleep. Two seats in front of her was a young girl, of about her own age, soft honey-coloured hair pulled into a bunch. She wore a pink scarf that a kind granny might have knitted for her, and pink gloves. She held a paperback book, a romantic classic of the last century, which Livvy had read and enjoyed in more innocent times. She reminded Livvy of her old self and of the last smart winter outfit she had had, the year her father died: a hat and cape of finest red wool trimmed with white fur, and a white fur muff on a red cord. She had worn boots lined with sheepskin, white wool stockings and a plaid skirt. None of those things fitted her any more, though they must still be hanging with mothballs in a storage cupboard somewhere. Glyn Howell's cheap wool-mix scarf did nothing to keep her warm, though she tried to snuggle into it. And ahead of her, the girl continued placidly with her reading. Livvy envied her and thought of the warm and spacious house waiting for her.

The tram rumbled through several city stops, and into the wider, bleaker streets of the suburb. The man with the paper got off, and another man, small, bald and bespectacled got on. A cross-section of ordinary people hoping to be home before curfew, safe for the moment in the steamed-up, rumbling tram.

Then the tram stopped again. Livvy sensed rather than heard a commotion downstairs. She turned round to see a group of soldiers, in a uniform she couldn't place. They seemed very big; they were laughing, and probably a bit drunk.

Their arrival caused a fluster of activity. Some people pulled out passes; some rose to their feet as if to get off the tram. But one of the soldiers stayed blocking the stairs. The young girl stayed fixed to her book, her pale face calm and trusting.

The men lurched up the aisle, once. Then down, looking from side to side as they went. When they came to the girl, they stopped, four big brutes, bull necks, red faces, tattooed arms. She looked up suddenly, and the trust went from her face.

In the confusion of the next few minutes, they had yanked her to her feet and were hauling her down the stairs. She had gasped, opened her mouth, but the protest had died on her lips. Everyone turned to see what was happening, then turned away, gazes fixed expressionlessly ahead. Livvy had half risen to protest, but then she too, had sat down again. 'Please!' the girl called out in a soft, strangled little voice. 'Please! No! Someone . . . Please don't!' Nobody answered. Nobody looked up again.

The girl was hauled off the bus, the tram started off, and everyone sat there, each locked in an individual shame.

*I should have protested*, thought Livvy guiltily. But if she had, what then? They'd probably have taken her too, just out of spite, and then, if they'd found out who she really was . . .

No, she could not, out of self defence, have acted any other way. But she felt sick to her stomach.

When she got off the tram, she ran, partly to beat the curfew, partly to try and shake off the guilt. That girl – what were they doing to her now? What kind of place had her country become?

The curfew siren sounded when she was still a couple of streets away from the old ladies' house. She ran and ran, and arrived at the door breathless.

In the living room, two faces looked up at her. Neither seemed anxious that she was late, and the smile on Miss Macdonald's face suggested she was hiding something, and biding her time before telling what it was.

Soon, though, it came out. 'You missed your boy-friend,' she said, almost in triumph.

'What do you mean?'

'That young lad who came with you. He stopped by, soon after you left. Said he had to get back, but he left you a note.'

'Oh,' said Livvy. She waited for it to be presented but this was not Miss Lena's style. 'Do you have the note?' she said after a while.

'Sybil? Did you see what I did with that note?'

'No, miss, I didn't.'

Miss Lena rose slowly and complainingly to her feet. 'Well, I shall just have to look,' she said, picking up a handful of papers from the mantelpiece. 'I expect it's here somewhere.' And with excruciating slowness, she riffled through the pile. Livvy waited, jumping from foot to foot, trying not to look too impatient, in case Miss Lena stopped altogether. 'No, it doesn't seem to be here . . . Oh, I remember. On the sideboard, behind the biscuit tin.'

'I'll get it,' said Livvy with alacrity, before any more 'old lady' slowness could deprive her of her letter. She found it, behind the biscuit tin, just as Miss Lena had said and snatched it up.

'Where are you going?' said Miss Sybil. 'There are no fires upstairs, you know.'

And Livvy heard Miss Lena's cackle: 'I expect she wants to read her secrets in peace and quiet.'

By the poor light of a candle, in her cold little room, Livvy unfolded Cai's letter.

> Dear Livy
>
> Sorry I wasnt able to stay But we have to go back to Wroxeter tonight Dad has a rush job on but I want to see you again If your in Wroxeter leave a message at the Britania Salt Key its quite safe hope your oright I do want to see you
>
> love Cai

His handwriting, round, uneven and uncertain, shocked her. It showed her just what different worlds they came from, she with her beautiful handwriting and careful education, and he, probably hustled through, and out of, a cramped and under-funded poor people's school in a dingy back street.

She folded up the letter and went downstairs again. The air was filled with a damp smell of overboiled stew. Sybil wanted help with laying the table. The kitchen windows were steamed up and the smell made her feel slightly queasy. Miss Lena hobbled her way to the table, and Livvy dished out greasy plates.

'That all you're having?' said Miss Lena. 'Won't keep a fly alive on that.'

'I'm not hungry,' said Livvy. 'I mean, it's very nice, but . . .'

'Bad news from your boyfriend?' asked Miss Lena, shovelling down stew.

Livvy averted her eyes. 'No. I mean he's not really my boyfriend, but . . . something else has happened. I've got to go back to Wroxeter.'

Miss Lena's eyes narrowed. Impossible to read her feelings. 'But I thought that place was dangerous for you.'

'It is. But . . .'

'Then you should stay here. If it's just that lad you're chasing . . .'

'It's nothing to do with him. I just have to go back.'

'What's so important there?'

'Look, I don't want to tell you. It's better if you don't know. Really.'

And for the first time, Miss Lena looked genuinely concerned, as she placed her spoon in her plate of cooling stew. 'You shouldn't go back there, girl. For whatever reason. No-one'll come looking for you here. Stay until it's safe to go back.'

'That's just it,' said Livvy. 'If I don't go back now, then it'll never be safe.'


# 17

All around her was the smell of salt and oil and sewage, the shouting and jostling of men, the booming of steamers, the black forest of masts, a cold sour wind driving up from the ocean and the screams of foraging seagulls. With Cai, it had all seemed so exciting and challenging; but now, with soldiers and Military

Police much in evidence and nowhere to hide, it was a different experience. Of course she couldn't have travelled last night – too dangerous to risk being caught by curfew officers. Yet if she had arrived the previous evening, she might just have caught Cai and the *Diligence.* An old sailor had told her that the *Diligence* had left at first light this morning, and would be a good few hours now on its way. She must find some other way of getting back.

Surprisingly, the old ladies had seemed really sorry to see her go. Miss Lena had pressed money into her hand, and even the fearsome Sybil had produced a packet of unappetising sandwiches. She promised she'd get back in touch with them as soon as she could, and let them know how things had worked out for her. Livvy wondered whether it would turn out to be an empty promise, for it was impossible to imagine how the world would change with the Emperor's death. She didn't say that, though, just kissed Miss Lena's whiskery cheek and said she'd write as soon as she was able.

The newspapers were carrying stories of the Emperor's illness – a 'slight cold', 'no anxiety'. Since they didn't usually report such things, Livvy wondered if they were beginning a gentle countdown to the inevitable. The Emperor was old, and had been on the throne since the age of ten, when his father, the popular and young Emperor Titus V, had been assassinated. Cosseted by aides and regents through his childhood, Julian had gradually taken over the reins of government. Almost no-one alive now could remember a time when he had not been Emperor.

At school, they learned the stories of his wonderful battle campaigns, all of which happened so long ago that they were as almost as mythical as the wars of ancient Troy. His stern profile was on all the coins; his statue stood tall in every town square; his photograph or portrait engraving hung in every official building. He was everywhere and had been there for ever, but somehow this had the effect of making him seem less, rather than more, real. His name, too, called up his famous predecessor, the first Emperor Julian, who fifteen hundred years ago, had restored the ancient ways and the ancient gods to the Empire, after his uncle had tried to make it Christian. Christians practised an odd religion; their god had been executed as a criminal, and they were rumoured to drink blood. 'Thank your lucky stars,' Don used to say, 'that that crowd aren't in charge of the Empire, or heavens knows what we'd all be up to now.' The strange religion had survived for many years in the eastern Empire, the breakaway regime centred in Constantinople. It had shrunk to almost nothing now, surrounded by 'proper' Romans on one side and by the Mohammedan Empire on the other, a weird survival of an ancient and peculiar regime, a fragile buffer zone. Rome seemed stronger than ever, centred in the great many-walled city of New Rome, built impregnably in the south of Gaul after Old Rome had been sacked by vandals. The Empire had survived that, had conquered and incorporated those vandals and others since, and surely now could survive forever.

Don had been a patriot in his way, though he'd never force-fed them with propaganda. But he was proud of Rome and Roman ways, and the Emperor had never come in for serious criticism. It was impossible to know if what the *Bleiddiaid* had said about the weakness of the Empire was true, and that Julian had been only kept in power by an efficient and ruthless support system. How would you know? These things never got out of the muffled labyrinthine corridors and heavy doors of the great palace in New Rome where he lived and was now dying.

But something was happening – Livvy felt sure of it. Soldiers roaming the streets out of control and everyone so frightened that they dared not do anything even when a young girl was abducted from under their noses – things had never been like this before! Her father would never have supported such an Empire – he would not have received his Military Medal so proudly from a Governor who would condone such things. Something had changed in the machinery of things – something had gone wrong and was slipping fast out of control. And some people – more of them than anyone realised – knew that things were going to change and change violently. Those people were all to be found in the army. The army, which had always held the Empire together, was now fatally split – between those who knew whatever it was – and those who didn't.

But her father *had* known something. He'd found something out – she was convinced of it. She replayed in her mind what Milo had told her of the conversation between her father and Uncle Paul. She was sure her father had intended it as a joke – he was chatting to Uncle Paul in what he imagined was privacy. He would never have knowingly left her in sole charge of lethal information.

But he had – it seemed – said it, and though it was said in jest, it was true. She was the only one who knew him well enough to understand how his mind would work.

And if she was right, she now knew exactly where she would find that information though she had no idea of its nature. It was a place that was ridiculously simple – yet only she would know of it.

While she was thinking these tangled and difficult thoughts, she'd been wandering around the quaysides, not really seeing where she was. Now she came slap up against a fence surrounding a low brick building.

Lavish signs around the door told her where she had arrived. It was the ticket office for the great steamer *Marcus Aurelius*. And a boom and a blast of steam signified that the steamer, before her in the dock was now getting ready to make its journey up the ancient Wroxeter canal, the busy waterway that she'd travelled down with Cai only a week or so previously.

Sailors were rushing around. Baggage was being loaded, ropes were being hauled up, doors were being closed. People gathered on deck, while others stood by the fence ready to wave them goodbye. A barrier had gone up in front of the ticket office. The last ticket had been sold and the ship was only minutes away from departure.

Suddenly, she heard a squawk at her side. A taxi had just rattled onto the quayside behind her and disgorged a mound of expensive-looking luggage and an irate woman swathed in furs.

'Porter! porter!' squawked the woman. She clutched her handbag and looked around her frantically. 'Porter! Oh why is there never . . .?'

No, there were no porters to be seen. They all jostled around the gangplank and the quayside, waiting no doubt for last-minute tips. The woman was helpless without them, and the taxi had rattled away.

'Porter! Oh *blast* these wretched people! What *is* the matter with everyone!'

It was then that she spotted the plebeian lad in his drab winter clothes watching her with some amusement. How dare he? What else were the plebs for but to help a lady with her luggage? 'Oh, you!' she squeaked. 'Come here at once! Give me a hand!'

Livvy came over and hauled the two largest bags. The woman had to scoop up the rest herself. The bags were heavy, but Livvy was stronger now from hefting bundles on to the *Diligence* and sacks of garden rubbish around Miss Lena's garden. Somehow she managed to follow the woman, who, on a waft of fur and perfume, charged through the empty ticket office, through the barrier, where she fumbled in her handbag for her ticket, and waved it before an official (the lad behind her of course, hauling luggage, passed ticketless, invisible). Then across the quayside, and up the gangway. Another wave of her ticket. And again, the invisible lad behind her with the luggage. There was a boom of engines and a blast of steam. Livvy stood on deck.

Around her, passengers leaned over the railings, excitedly waiting to wave goodbye to their friends and families. Probably most of them were travelling home for the Solstice – there was an air of festival and excitement about the gathering in their bright clothes. They carried parcels, holly wreaths and champagne bottles. Sailors in their blue uniforms ran here and there, shouting and getting in people's way. The last porters heaved themselves off deck. 'Passengers only!' yelled a voice. 'Everyone else off!'

'Oh, come on, come on,' panicked the woman, though since she had boarded the boat in time, she had no more need to worry. She grabbed a sailor and demanded the way to her cabin. Off she went, clatter clatter in her silly high heels, across the deck. Livvy followed, hefting the bags, her arms about to fall off, her breath hurting in her chest.

But something gave her the strength, and she bumped and dragged the luggage – 'Careful, you dolt, those things are expensive!' – through walnut-panelled doors, down stairs, and along the cream-painted, carpeted curve of the first class corridor.

The woman reached her cabin and waited for Livvy to shove the door open. Livvy almost fell in, and dropped the heavy cases on the floor. The cabin was lapped in soft creamy colours, a cushiony armchair, a bunk piled high with feather pillows, silk cushions, a bowl of pink silk roses. 'What a nightmare!' moaned the woman. 'Oh dear. I'm exhausted!'

She turned to look at Livvy. For Livvy stood with her hand held out, as she had seen porters and waiters do. She didn't really need the tip, but she was damned if she was going to let this rich bitch get away without paying it.

'I suppose you want money! Though the way you dragged those cases . . .! Oh, very well. Here you are.'

And a trickle of bronze coins fell grudgingly into Livvy's hand. 'Thanks, ma'am,' said Livvy, the first time she'd spoken, and she dived off into the corridor, slamming the cabin door shut behind her.

She was on board the *Marcus Aurelius* and it was just about to start for Wroxeter.

# 18

She had to get away from the first class corridor and soon she was on deck again, among the swarm of sailors, cabin attendants, waiters and passengers. The official still called, more urgently now, for anyone who was not a passenger to disembark.

Leaving the first class deck, she found her way, down half a flight of steps, to the steerage deck, where even more passengers milled around, and leaned over the rail. 'She's off!' somebody called, and Livvy saw the gangplank being wheeled away. With a great boom, the *Marcus Aurelius* began to move, and Livvy, joining the excited surge by the railings, saw the gap between rail and quay gradually widening, and the grey water swirling and rocking around her. Everyone was waving to someone, and she waved too, to no-one. The gap grew, so that now a steady channel of water and the dark buildings of London began to slip past her, towers and walls and pointed roofs and chimneys.

Soon they were out in the wider reaches of the Thames, distant blocks of docks and steamers from exotic locations and the scent of spices drifting across from the great warehouses. Then the boat began to turn sharply, and veered into what she now knew was the Wroxeter canal basin, slipping between suburban walls, trees and bleak parks. Gradually the watchers peeled away from the rail and went down into the warmth below decks.

Livvy stayed until she felt she would have attracted attention by staying, and then she too went downstairs. The steerage rooms were cramped and dark. People sat crammed on wooden benches, those at the ends peering out through little portholes. Doors swung open onto smelly lavatories, smokers were jammed into a corridor, and others queued for ham rolls and tea served from a kiosk tucked into a corner. There was a bar, where men played pinball, or cards, drank beer or listened to the racing on the radio. Livvy forgot she could pass among them unnoticed, and as always it surprised her, no-one staring or ogling her or making suggestive comments.

But she didn't want to take her invisibility for granted. She would be on this boat for a couple of days after all, and she would have to be careful not to make herself conspicuous.

A couple of hours into the journey, she realised just how careful she was going to have to be. A uniformed inspector was passing through the bar. 'Tickets please!' he called. 'All steerage passengers, tickets and passes ready please!'

Livvy looked around her frantically. The inspector was bent down now over a group of men. She slipped out of the bar and into the corridor. She pushed open the door of the toilets. Three women and two small children were standing by the washbasins, washing hands and combing their hair. When they saw Livvy, they stopped and stared at her.

'What do you think you're doing?' called one of them. 'Out! Now!'

Oops. Yes. She'd forgotten again. Muttering an apology, she slipped out. The door to the Gents was propped open by a couple of men with black-and-white Chester scarves, talking loudly and drunkenly. A smell of urine and vomit wafted out at her. Of course she could have gone in, locked herself in a cubicle and waited for a reasonable time, but she just couldn't bring herself to do it. There had to be another way of avoiding the inspector.

Easing her way back into the crowded main cabin, where steerage passengers were packed on benches, Livvy found a gap at the end of a bench occupied by a weary mother with five small children. She clutched a baby and a two-year-old on her lap, two little girls wriggled and fidgeted, and a boy of about four screamed and squirmed and kicked everything in sight. 'Oh, Kevin, just stop your nonsense, will you?' the woman said. But Kevin was immune to her appeals. The baby in her lap started to wriggle.

Livvy had always found that, although she didn't like small children very much, she was good with them. She'd once kept a crowd of badly-behaved brats entranced at a summer barbecue party way back in the old days. So she reached across and grabbed little Kevin firmly. 'Shall I hold him for you?' she asked the mother across the row of writhing little bodies, and the woman was too exhausted to do anything but nod in gratitude.

Livvy pulled little Kevin onto her lap, swaddled his kicking limbs firmly with her arms, and hissed, 'If you shut up, I'll tell you a story about a monster!' Kevin yelled loudly that he didn't want to hear about no mon . . . What monster? Livvy knew she had won and launched into a lurid tale about a blood-sucking, children-crunching ogre. Soon Kevin was silent, and both little girls were clutching her arm in enjoyable horror.

And all this time, she was aware of the ticket inspector making his way up the cabin. When he came to the mother, he stopped, and she fished awkwardly in her bag, while the babies squirmed in her arms. The inspector took pity on her, and dismissed her as soon as he glimpsed the orange edge of her steerage ticket and the tattered wallet of papers. He did not stop to account for all of her children, least of all the boy who was sitting among a mass of little ones at the far end of the bench.

Livvy finished the story anyway, which ended with a bad little boy being Eaten Right Up! Crunch! Crunch! Crunch! This particular little boy giggled and then said anxiously, 'Wasn't a really monster, was it?' Livvy was so grateful to him for saving her from the inspector, that she gave him a kiss and said, 'No, course not. Monsters don't eat little boys.'

At Leicester the *Marcus Aurelius* stopped for an hour, to lose some passengers and pick up others. By then it was night-time, and Livvy ate Sybil's dry meat-paste sandwiches (something she would have been far too grand to touch in the days when a cook and a kitchen maid prepared dainty meals for the family) and tried to sleep on a hard bench. Men who'd been drinking lurched noisily in from the bar; children fretted and cried. Livvy thought longingly of how the cross lady in furs was sleeping, lapped in her soft sheets, something brought to her on a tray. Grilled salmon, perhaps, thought Livvy hungrily. Or chicken salad. Or fresh pasta with meat sauce . . . She dozed fitfully and hungrily, and dreamed of food.

In the mid-morning, she saw the ticket inspector again. She hurried to the toilets (she'd had to use the smelly Gents, eventually, last night) but this morning there was another bossy little man in uniform there standing by the door. 'Toilets closed, sir,' he said, 'until after ticket inspection.' Clearly others had had the same idea.

She pushed her way back into the dark steerage cabin, and looked for the downtrodden woman with her children. They were quieter this morning. Little Kevin slept with his head in his sister's lap, the little girls sucked their thumbs, and the baby slept. Livvy eased herself into a gap, next to the mother. 'Hello, dear,' said the woman, recognising her.

'Could you do me a favour?' Livvy whispered. 'I haven't done anything wrong, but I don't have a ticket. I want to go home to see my mother for the Solstice.' Which was true, in a way. 'I don't want you to lie for me, but if I could just sit at the end with your little ones, they might not notice me.'

It was probably the bit about seeing her mother that did it. 'I'm sure she's wanting to see you,' said the woman. 'Yes, of course. You sit at the end. Kevin'll be glad. He's been asking all night when the gentleman who told the stories will be coming back.'

This time, Livvy managed an even more complicated tale about a boy who got blown up to the size of a house and floated up to the South Pole. Livvy piled on angry seagulls and jagged icebergs and hungry bears. If I ever get out of this, she thought, I've got a great career as a children's story-writer. And once again the ticket inspector passed her by.

And so it was that at about lunch-time the *Marcus Aurelius* steamed through the intense greenness of the Cornovian plains beneath a misty winter sky, the air scented with fog and woodsmoke, through the crowded suburbs with a distant glitter of towers and pinnacles, into the docks at Wroxeter.

# 19

The quayside was a scene of family reunions and laughter and huggings and shoutings, exclaimings over parcels and presents. It seemed that she was the only one who didn't have someone joyfully waiting for her. Yet oddly, she now felt more relaxed, as though, in her home city, she could be more in control of events.

Though just how tricky Wroxeter was going to be was brought home to her as she made her way through the harbour buildings. A big poster was pinned to the wall among the advertisements for cough syrup and ladies' corsets; a blurred picture of someone who seemed slightly familiar looked out wistfully from a mass of big black print.

HAVE YOU SEEN THIS GIRL?

And a request to inform the Military Police of any sightings.

She wondered where they'd found the picture, which she now recognised as one taken the year her father died. She'd not had another one taken since, and she knew that she must look different from the wide-eyed twelve-year-old, from whom she now turned her eyes.

But on the other hand, they were still looking for a girl, which meant that Don's plans for her had so far succeeded. As to whether the *Bleiddiaid* knew where she was, there was no way of telling. She certainly didn't want to encounter them again.

She made her way in and out of the dingy quayside streets and alleys until she found Salt Quay. The Britannia was a little pub squashed between two larger buildings, so narrow that she almost walked past it.

She entered through a low doorway into a passage

smelling of beer, and then into a dark oddly-shaped bar-room. There was nothing fancy about the Britannia – just a basic ale-house: a bar with a row of pump handles, an old-fashioned till and a row of glasses. A couple of men were drinking and a barman, skinny as a weasel, was drying glasses. The air was thick with smoke and beer fumes. The men flickered bored glances over her as she entered, and returned to their conversation about a wrestling match. The barman threw in an odd word, 'He's not on form, the Strangler isn't – not a match for Thunderer – you'll see. Yes?'

This was addressed to Livvy, as she came up to the bar. Livvy coughed and summoned up her boy's throaty voice. 'A mate of mine said I could leave a message here for him.'

'Oh, yeah? What name?'

'Cai. Cai Llewelyn.'

The man's eyes flickered, just for a moment. 'Oh, yeah. Well, if I see him, what'll I say?'

'Just that – Glyn – I'm back – in Wroxeter. I'll look for him tonight, maybe. Or tomorrow night.'

'I'll tell him.' The barman slammed down a glass. 'If he's in.'

The two men broke off their conversation. 'His old man'll be here most likely. Never far from the booze, old Dai.'

'Yeah, well don't tell *him*,' said Livvy anxiously. 'Just Cai. If he's around.'

'I'll do that. Drink while you're here?'

'Bit young for the booze, isn't he?' said one of the men. 'Get you into trouble.'

'I don't want a drink,' said Livvy hurriedly. 'Just the message if that's OK. Thanks.'

134

And she left the bar and was outside again.

The posters were everywhere. Some had been scrawled over, with glasses and a moustache added, or obscene comments. Others had already been half obliterated by fly-posters advertising cheap alcohol, or a post-Solstice party in some dingy cellar. But certainly the inhabitants of Wroxeter had plenty of time to have studied her twelve-year-old face. Poor little thing, they'd be thinking. Or spoiled hussy – however they reacted, they'd want to find her and return her to the bosom of her loving, grieving family.

But it seemed to her as she made her way into the crowded centre of the city that today, the Solstice celebrations were what most people had on their minds, as they staggered home under the weight of shopping. Candles and holly branches decorated shop windows, and the bakeries were warm with the spicy smell of Winterbread – the rich spiced cake only made at this time of year. Livvy had always loved the Solstice – the warmth and the lights and the sudden flowering of green branches in the dead season of the year. It was an especially British festival – in the warm south of Gaul or Iberia they didn't need to cheer themselves up during the short, dark days, or to weave spells that ensured the bright days of spring were on their way. Of course, Livvy's family hadn't had much to celebrate since her father died – but she could still remember what fun the Solstice had been, her father coming home a little earlier than usual from the barracks, laughing and mysterious, to the house that Livvy and her mother had decorated with green branches; the scent of mulled wine, the presents that suddenly and mysteriously emerged wrapped in gold paper, the servants giggly and grateful, even Tony relaxed and smiling. Then they'd hear the thunderous knock on the door that indicated the arrival of the *Mari Lwyd*, that strange old custom, with men dressed up and carrying a stick decorated to look like a horse's head, shouting their raucous song with a mixture of deference and defiance, while her father showered silver coins into the bag that they held out. You could be sure, Tony said disapprovingly, that wives and families would never catch sight of those coins and only the pubs would benefit, but Livvy's father cuffed him affectionately round the side of the head and said, 'Loosen up, Tony!' – the last person who could say that to her brother and get away with it.

That was the Solstice – in the old days! This year, her Solstice looked like being lonely and scary, she thought, as she left the crowded shopping precinct, and arrived at the familiar quiet tree-lined streets of her old district. How odd to be back here – only a few weeks since she'd left to go to Ishtar, but everything had that disconcerting air of weird familiarity and familiar strangeness that comes after absence. She noted how the streets looked dingy: paintwork was peeling and chipped; there was something sad about the big villas hidden behind high walls in the old Roman way. The modern style was to have brash and elegant front gardens, pillars and windows and shrubs and statues and gilded paint, all your wealth on show. It had been a point of honour, her father used to say, with Romans of the old school, to be discreet about their possessions, as though somehow it made wealth classier to be hidden.

But they looked sad and lost, these old half-hidden villas, under the grey winter sky – they were silent and showed no signs of life, except for the occasional barking of a dog, set off by her passing.

Here was Tiber Avenue, where Max had lived. She turned the corner by a huge old maple tree which still had some scraps of tawny leaves clinging to the bare branches, into Alban Avenue, with the park bench on which the old veterans would sit by the hour, sipping from flasks of whisky-laced coffee and discussing the old days. Here was the house where the aging actress had lived – the small boys used to laugh as she trailed her fur coats and three little dogs with jewelled collars, her face a mask of white foundation and blackened wild spider-leg eyes. She'd died the previous year, and a wealthy builder had moved in, and had plonked a row of garishly-painted busts along the outside wall, to the disgust of the neighbours. Livvy turned at last into her own road, Aventine Close, even quieter than the rest, an elegant cul-de-sac of half a dozen two hundred-year-old houses, all hidden behind high plastered walls, each with a heavy door set with a huge bronze knocker and a bell-pull, which would sound in the depths of the house and send a servant rushing to open it.

The trees had lost most of their leaves since she'd last been there, and there was rubbish piled up outside some of the doors, suggesting that tomorrow was the last dustbin day before the Solstice. The pavements were swept and clean, but the plasterwork of the walls was peeling and scabby, she noticed. And there at the far end, her own house, tucked into the corner, with the tall cypress tree and the ivy trailing down.

Locked and deserted, Don had said – but surely that street door was half open. Yes! And as she approached, she could hear voices. She quickened her pace, and her heart began to beat nervously.

The door was flung wide open. A man came out, with

a sack of rubbish. He wore the dark jacket of a house servant, but he wasn't Llew, or Morgan . . . He was tall, and thin with a beaked nose, bald except for a rim of curly hair around his ears. He was no-one she recognised. She had stopped still, and he didn't see her. Instead, he disappeared back into the yard.

Livvy came closer, nervously now. Here was the wall she knew so well, with the thin rim of slate tiles at the top, the scuffing at the foot, the rusty bronze grille where Tony used to tease her that a dragon lived. Did Tony ever tease? Yes, yes, he did, a long time ago. It was all a long time ago. There were the marks where someone had fly-posted an election poster, which Llew had torn down. There was the house number – a discreet 'IV' set in a blue tile.

And here another notice – a new, cheap wooden plaque pinned to the plaster: BEWARE OF THE DOG, it said. But they had no dog. What did it mean?

And then, there was a scuffling and a rattling. A small boy emerged, pedalling a three-wheeler bike. He had a small round face, with curly black hair, and little black boot-button eyes. He stared up at Livvy with cold self-assurance.

'Who are you?' said Livvy breathlessly.

'Timmy, of course,' he said pityingly. 'Who are you?'

'What are you doing here?'

'I live here, *stupid*.'

'But . . . but how long have you lived here, I mean . . .'

'We've *always* lived here,' he said, and began to steer the bike out into the pavement, almost aiming at Livvy, who had to jump out of his way. He started to ride around in a determined, vicious little arc, his small jaw set, the arrogance of one who had not yet found out that the world didn't revolve around him. 'This is my *old* bike,' he announced. 'I'm getting a much better one for the Solstice.' Then the gate swung open again, and a woman dashed out. She wore a sensible dark blue woollen dress, and her hair was tucked back into a bun. Livvy's own nanny had dressed just like this. 'Master Timothy! Get inside at once! You know you're not supposed to play in the street!' As if to echo her, a barking dog set up its cacophony from inside the house.

The woman shot an angry, suspicious glance at Livvy. 'Who are you? If I see you hanging around again, I'll get the police on to you! Go away!'

And within a few seconds, Master Timothy, his nurse and his bike had disappeared behind the garden door, which then slammed shut. She could imagine them clearly, in the little paved yard, lined with rows of neatly clipped shrubs in terracotta pots, then going up the two wide steps that led to the front door of the house, between its two Corinthian columns, into the vestibule with the marble floor . . . she could see it all so precisely. These people, whoever they were, didn't live here, did they? *She* lived here, with her mother and Llew and Minna and all the rest of the faces she knew . . .

And from inside the house, the barking dog – who also didn't live there – continued its warning cry.

## 20

She'd intended to get inside the house, even if it was empty as Don had said, find what she believed was still hidden there, and then lie low for a few days while she considered her options. But it was as though *they* had

139

even anticipated that. Someone else now lived in her house, and had always lived there, if the cocky little boy was to be believed.

Well – that particular plan was not on. But all was not lost. There was a way in around the back – she used to use it sometimes when she'd gone out with Max, and wanted to avoid her mother and Tony finding out. It was a burglar's way, really; she would have to be a burglar in her own house.

So she turned into the next road, by the neighbourhood hall, where meetings and concerts were sometimes held. A narrow passage went down behind the hall, round a dark corner – and around the back of her garden. The wall was high at the back, but there was one place – a corner – where a couple of loose stones made a foothold, and you could scramble down the other side on to a garden bench. Livvy looked furtively around her. But on this wintery afternoon, everything was quiet. Sometimes she had hated the almost unearthly silence of their neighbourhood – but today she blessed it.

Some weeds had pushed up impertinent leaves at the base of the wall that ran along the passage, a cat ran past her in a flash of black fur, but otherwise there was nothing to see, or hear. Tall walls reared up on either side. She marked them as she passed. Here was their neighbour's garden. And here, hers began.

A tree dipped over the wall, bare branches hanging like black hair. She remembered how and where it had been planted, in a semicircle at the far end, decorative tiles around the base.

And here they were – the missing stones in the wall. Max had always helped her climb up in the past. But she was taller now, and stronger. She rubbed her hands together, gave a little cough, just to psych herself up, wedged a foot into the lowest gap and hauled herself up by the jutting stone. Another foot, and she was able to lift herself up to the top of the wall.

The garden – her garden – spread below her, with its network of paths, the dense shading of shrubs. She saw how neglected the paths were, how unswept leaves lay thick on the ground. She could see the fountain, dried up and empty now, and just around the corner, the pillared base of the bust of Minerva . . .

And then suddenly an explosion of noise burst out, and hurtling through a bush, round a corner, and directly up the path below her, the biggest ugliest mastiff she'd ever seen. *Beware of the dog*, the sign had said, and this creature, with its slavering jaws and huge strong limbs, was a dog to beware of, all right.

So near and so far . . . She stared at it for a few seconds, and then realising that the noise would probably attract someone from inside the house, scrambled back down the wall and dropped to the ground. Then, not caring whether anyone noticed her or not, nor how suspicious it looked, she ran. Ran and ran, out of the quiet streets, down pavements and across roads, past houses and trees and gardens and shops, until she had left her district behind her.

Panting now, she leaned against a wall. But she could not stay here long. This was a busy road. A steam tram rattled by in a sulphury cloud. Carts rumbled over the stones; bicycles swerved to avoid shoppers. It was getting dark now, and she was glad of it. But the streets were still full, and Wroxeter still seethed with people. Colours were draining away fast in the thickening air, lights were blossoming in windows and pedestrians were reduced to a blur of hunched shapes and muted tones. She was able to slip in and out of them, still, she hoped, unnoticed. Even her face on the posters was growing indistinct now. Smoke caught in her throat as evening fires were lit in countless houses.

She retraced her steps back to the dockside area, streets becoming narrower, filled with the smells of bad drains, or cigarettes, of sausages and kebabs being grilled in greasy cafés. Street led into street. She could smell the canal now, the sour water.

Then she saw a shape coming into focus, moving briskly up the road. His head was cast down; his hands were in his pockets; he moved with grim determination and purpose. She could not believe that he was here, just like that, after all the trouble she'd had getting here, that they'd simply bump into each other.

He stopped and she stopped. As it had been when she'd returned to her house, he too looked subtly different from how she'd pictured him. Probably she'd been confusing his image in her mind with that of Max. Cai was shorter than she'd remembered, and broader in the chest; and the narrow tattooed band on his brow surprised her all over again. 'Oh, Cai!' she cried, half in joy, half in misery. In a couple of quick paces, he had reached her.

'Livvy!' he said, 'it's great to see you,' and suddenly his arms were round her and he was kissing her on the lips. As she plunged her hands into his rough wool jersey, and smelled his smell, he became familiar again.

Her first kiss, too, she thought, as though part of her was surveying this from above, taking in the unfamiliar sensation of someone so close to her, the feel of his clothes, the texture of his skin, the warmth of his breath.

She wanted to stay like this for ever, but then a thought struck her and she pulled away. 'Cai,' she said, 'you've just been kissing a . . . a . . . *bloke!*'

He pulled away too. Then he laughed. 'Who cares?' he said, and made as if to kiss her again. But he only held her for a second this time, and then let his arms drop. 'I never thought I'd see you again. What are you doing here?'

'It's a long story,' she said. 'And . . .'

'Don't tell me now. We'll go somewhere quiet. They gave me your message, but I didn't want to take you back there – you can't hear yourself think in that place.'

'But where can we go?'

'Well,' he said. 'Where had you meant to go?'

'My old house,' she said. 'But I can't go back. That's part of the long story.'

'Hmm.' Then, 'You're coming with me.'

'Where?'

'My house of course.'

'*Your* house?'

'Got a better plan?'

'No. But your dad . . .'

'My dad does what he's told, at home. You haven't met my ma.'

'Yes, but . . .'

'Frightened of slumming it, is that it?'

'No, of course not, but . . .'

'I've never kissed a posh girl before,' he said with a grin. 'Bet you've never kissed anyone as rough as me, either.'

'Well . . .' she began, and decided to tell the truth. 'I've never actually kissed *anyone* before, Cai. Not like that.'

He turned in surprise. 'Well, what a sheltered young lady you are! My sisters had their first babies by the time they were your age.'

'Don't make fun of me.'

'I'm not,' he said seriously. 'I'm really not. When I think of all you've been through, and the way you were brought up, I'm impressed. Really, Liv. I've never met anyone like you before.'

Probably it was just flattery. Probably he didn't mean it. But she couldn't stop his words running through her head and she couldn't stop them making her glow. *I've never met anyone like you before . . .*


# 21

Cai's house stood in a workers' estate by the docks, row upon row of little red-brick houses, in narrow grids of streets. They had no front gardens, and, it seemed to Livia, were impossibly small, like shabby dolls' houses. The smells of cooking and gritty coal smoke drifted out. 'In you go, Livia Marcel,' he said. The front door was so low and so narrow, she felt she was squeezing herself in. A dark little hallway – scuffed carpet on dark lino, a few drab prints on the walls, and then a cloud of steam coming out at them. Cai walked into the steam, which came from a room hung with white sheets like a multitude of ghosts. A tiny dark woman in a flowered overall was ironing in the middle of it all. 'Oh, there you are,' she said, as Cai came into the room. 'I wanted you to . . . Who's he?' she broke off suddenly, staring at Livvy with dark little screwed-up eyes. She did not look at all friendly. Livvy's heart sank. Was this was going to be as bad as the Misses Lena and Sybil?

Cai gave her a kiss. 'Hold your horses, Ma, and don't say anything till I've finished. This isn't a boy. It's a girl. She's Livia Marcel, and she's dressed like this because the Scum are after her. She's not done anything wrong, but she's afraid if they get her, they'll kill her. I want you, dear Ma, to let her stay for a few days, right?'

Cai's mother put down her iron. 'Now wait a minute . . .' she said. Then she peered at Livvy in sudden recognition. 'You're the girl in the posters, aren't you? So how come you end up with my son? Why should I help you?'

'It's a long story, Ma, and she hasn't told me all of it herself. But I do trust her, and you can too.' His tone was soft, caressing almost, and she took his hand as she thought it over.

'I don't want any trouble,' she said.

'You won't, Ma. Not if we all stay quiet.'

'Oh, yeah?' she said. 'Your dad'll stay quiet, will he?'

'He's already met Livia. He thinks she's a boy called Glyn.'

Livvy listened to the to-and-fro of the conversation with some surprise. It was more civilised than her mother and Tony would have been. Tony would harangue; her mother would moan. In spite of the roughness of her tone, there was real affection in Cai's mother's voice. Livvy realised how chill and distant her own family life seemed in comparison.

When Cai had finished telling his side of her story, she tried to explain about Ishtar, and how she was trapped there, being fattened up for a forced marriage.

Then she told of her suspicions that her mother had been hidden away in a home for drug addicts. Mrs Llewelyn's eyes sharpened at that. Mothers responded to injustices inflicted on mothers. 'Poor soul,' she said. 'And your father was a good man, you say?'

'He was the best.'

'Huh,' she said. 'They could dispose of my old man, and we'd all be better off. No, that's not fair. I'd miss the old rogue sometimes. But it sounds like you've had a tough time of it.'

'She has,' said Cai, 'which is why I want you to . . .'

'All right,' snapped Mrs Llewelyn, 'you've made your point. I don't mind you staying for a bit. But you can't stay in hiding forever. What will you do next?'

Livvy couldn't tell her that. But she said, 'If I can get back to London, and get to see the Governor, he might put things right.'

'The Governor! You can just walk in and see him, can you?'

'My father was a hero. The Governor knows who I am. If I could only get to him, I'm sure he'd listen.'

Mrs Llewelyn picked up the iron and glared at its hot surface, as if she wished to hit a Roman over the head with it. 'Well, you certainly move in high circles, girl. Folks like us don't get to walk in on the Governor, no matter what things they've done to us. Well. All right. You can stay for a bit, just over the Solstice. But then you'll have to sort yourself out.'

'That's really kind of you. I . . .'

'The old man's got a mouth like a drain. He'll be told to shut up, but he won't shut up forever, not after a few drinks. So mind you don't put us at risk any more than you have to.'

146

'I'm really . . .'

'And you!' She plonked the iron down on the top of the range where it hissed like an angry snake, and turned to her son. 'She sleeps in her room; you sleep in yours. No nonsense, mind. Nothing like that goes on in my house, you understand?'

Livvy blushed and Cai hid his face in his hands and groaned 'Ma-a!' in mock embarrassment. But he said, 'Yes, Ma, I understand.'

Very soon, Cai's dad came home, having finished one drinking session and getting himself geared up for the next. As far as he was concerned, the thin boy whom his son had brought home was the useless beggar they'd had on the boat the other week. No-one was inclined to disillusion him. He railed at Cai for bringing boys home, and told him that if he turned out to be a bloody poof, he'd kick him out the bloody door, he would. Cai said that if he tried, he'd kick him out first. Livvy sat uncomfortably on a horsehair couch in a corner of the cramped little sitting room, clutching a bowl of soup. Mrs Llewelyn looked at her observing all this, and said, 'He's not bad when he's sober. But Solstice is a bad time for us all. Cai told you about Bran, did he?'

Livvy nodded.

'Happened about this time of the year. You can guess what kind of a Solstice we had that year.' She sighed, and said nothing for a while.

Cai's father went back to the pub eventually, and his mother took out some darning. Livvy sat still and quiet most of the time, letting warmth and food seep though her. She was tired but didn't want to sleep. Cai's presence in the room was like an electric hum: though she didn't look at him all the time, she couldn't stop thinking about him. And all the time, the other bit of her, the dispassionate observer, who had watched over the last few weeks with sceptical fascination, was thinking, *Livvy, you don't need this, you don't need all these feelings, what with everything else you've got on your plate . . .*

It was not late when Mrs Llewelyn folded her mending and announced that she was off to bed. She shot a look at Cai, whose meaning could not be mistaken, and Cai responded with a resigned shrug. 'All right, Ma. Don't worry.'

Then she was gone, and the two were alone in the room. Cai immediately jumped up and came to sit next to her on the horsehair couch. 'No-one says I have to sit a million miles away,' he said as he took her hand. 'I can hear you much better like this.'

'Oh, Cai,' she said, 'I've got so much to tell you. I don't know where to start.'

'The beginning is usually the best place. So let's go from you knocking at that mad old lady's door and take it from there.'


# 22

And so she told him. She started with Misses Lena and Sybil, and that made him laugh. But he didn't laugh when she described her trip to the flea market and how the nameless couple – the resistance, the terrorists, whoever they were – had confronted her. Then she went on to describe her journey across town and her meeting with

Milo. She told of the anarchic feeling in London, and of the girl who was snatched from a tram in full view of the passengers. She told him how she'd sneaked aboard the *Marcus Aurelius* and avoided the ticket collector. He smiled at that. 'You're learning, Liv. You're learning!'

And finally, she described her visit to her old house, and what she'd found there. In a way, that was the end of the story, because nothing else had happened. But . . .

He gave her a sharp look.

'Go on. What else?'

'That's it, really.'

'No, it isn't.'

She sighed. 'No, it isn't. But . . .'

The *but* was that from here on, all was guess work and a memory of a conversation she'd had just over three years ago, in her garden, in that very hot summer that had marked the end of her father's life.

She'd been helping him cut back the overgrown ivy. It had massed over the back wall, was creeping along the paths and was threatening to smother every bush in the garden. He was wearing his ordinary clothes – sand-coloured trousers and an open-necked white shirt. A ragged old straw hat was perched on his head. You certainly wouldn't have taken him for a senior army officer. And she was in an old cotton dress, her long hair caught back in a pigtail. Together, with secateurs and shears, they pulled off great swathes of ivy and piled it up to be burned.

And at some point, her father had noticed the ivy working its way over and around the old statue of Minerva. Minerva, grave under her helmet, was covered in green tendrils and they'd even found their way under the base of the statue.

149

'If I lift,' he'd said, 'will you pull away the stuff that's grown under her?'

And he'd taken the bust in his arms, and tilted it, while she pulled the ivy away.

It was then she'd noticed it. 'Daddy, Minerva's hollow inside!' For she had always imagined her to be solid stone.

'Why, so she is.'

'No-one would guess,' said twelve-year-old Livvy, 'that there was a space inside, would they? We always said Minerva knew all our secrets. Wouldn't it be a great place to hide them?'

He'd laughed. 'You have a wild imagination, Miss Marcel.'

'No, but wouldn't it? If I had a secret I wanted to hide from everyone, I'd leave it there, wouldn't you?'

And she remembered that suddenly he'd looked at her in a different way, his face divided into sharp planes in the sunlight, the ragged shadow of his hat bisecting his forehead.

'Yes,' he said, quietly. 'Maybe I just would.'

When she told this to Cai now, it sounded stupid, but he didn't laugh, just sat staring quietly into the dying fire. She tried to put it all together so it made sense.

'What I think now . . . what I've been trying to work out for the last few days . . . is that my father was putting together some sort of dossier. And he'd got something – something important, but it wasn't quite enough to take to the Governor.'

'But he had to put this important information somewhere safe?'

'Exactly. He couldn't keep it in his office in the barracks, because he didn't know who he could trust. Couldn't put it in the house because even the servants might be bribed. And the bank, his lawyer, all those people . . . we just don't know who's in the conspiracy.'

'Must be a lot of them,' mused Cai, 'if they're planning to overthrow the government. Lurking everywhere, just waiting. Scary, that.'

'It's horrible,' said Livvy. 'I don't even want to think about it, and now I have to.' She shuddered. 'And I'm so tired. I just want to sleep for a week.'

'Maybe that's what you'd better do,' said Cai. 'Till tomorrow anyway. Come on, Glyn Howells. I'll show you your room.'

And sleep she did, hardly noticing what the room was like, except that, as soon as her head touched the pillow, she was sucked down and down into the deepest sleep imaginable. Her dreams were confused and disturbing, about appointments being missed and homework not being done, her mother annoyed with her, and somehow, in the middle of it, her father smiling at her from behind a door, which then closed upon him . . . But it was the first time in weeks that she'd slept like this, dead to the world.

She was awoken, centuries later, it seemed, into bright cold daylight, and Cai bringing her a cup of tea. She sat up in bed, and rubbed her eyes. It was a tiny attic room, she now saw, with no furniture except a rickety table by the bed, and a wooden chair, over which some of Glyn Howells's rough outer garments were now thrown.

'I can't hang around,' said Cai, kissing her lightly on the forehead, 'or Ma will be up with the rolling pin, but I thought I'd just say good morning, and Happy Solstice.'

'I'd forgotten it was Solstice today. Ouch. I feel really scuzzy. I'd just love a bath.'

Cai laughed. 'I bet you would. And so would we. You'll have to go to the bathhouse for that, miss. Not something I'd recommend in your present condition. Oh, and the toilet's outside in the yard. Life among the plebs.'

'I'm sorry,' said Livvy. 'I don't want to sound fussy. But some cold water to wash my face . . .'

'Will be done. Did you sleep well?'

'Better than I've slept for ages.'

'Then we must be doing something right. I'll bring you the water, and then you can come down for breakfast. Dad's gone off to the racing, so we're shot of him. And Ma's chatting to her cronies up the road.'

'Won't you be getting ready for Solstice?'

'Not in this house we won't. Ma'll be lighting candles for Bran later on. That's all the Solstice we'll have.'

'Won't your sisters be here?'

'Not this year. Bron's up in the north and can't get the papers, and Cait's oldest is sick and she'll be staying at home. We don't go a bundle on the Solstice anyway.'

'I'm sorry.'

'No need to be.' He got up. 'I'll fetch your water.'

Later, washed and as clean as she could be in clothes that she'd worn non-stop for days, she went downstairs to find Cai and they picked up their conversation of the previous night.

'So what's next, Liv?'

'I've got to get inside my garden, somehow. And find out whatever it is. But I just don't know how to. Not with that dog.'

Cai thought about it. 'Well, this evening, the streets'll be full of people, all masked and dressed up. And

152

because it's the Solstice, there won't be a curfew. It's our best chance of getting over there without anyone noticing.'

She noticed that he'd said 'us'. 'I can't ask you to come with me,' she said.

'I'm not having you doing all that on your own.'

'I have to do it, but you don't. Why risk yourself?'

He shrugged. 'I'm sick of things as they are, up and down the canal all day. There must be something more to life than this. If I don't try, I'll never know.'

'But if we get caught . . .'

He grinned. 'I've no intention of getting caught. Nor will you. You'll see.'

'This isn't a children's game, Cai.'

'We're not children any more. Call it my revenge for Bran. If I can do anything to make things hard for the Scum, I'll do it.'

Livvy wasn't sure that was what she wanted. Did she want to overturn the way of life she'd known for so long? Part of her did, because it was starting to feel like a life full of cracks and fissures. But part of her wanted still to be that young girl who had nothing more to worry about other than being late for violin lessons, and making sure parents didn't find out about Don's drinking habits. Yet that life was over anyway. And it would be comforting to have Cai with her, whatever his motives.

'What about that dog? He looked ready to tear my throat out.'

'I'll see to the dog, don't worry.'

'But don't hurt him!'

'A tranquilliser,' he said patiently. 'Mate of mine works at the dog-track. Knows how to shut them up for a while if he needs to.'

153

'Is it legal?'

Cai laughed. 'Course it's not legal. But then neither is breaking and entering. I told you, leave the dog to me.'

So that was it. Tonight it was, then.

# 23

Music was playing raucously from a barrel organ somewhere, and the streets were full of people. Some carried tall candles, ivy-wreathed, shading them against the wind. Others had brass lanterns. Many wore masks – the authorities didn't like it, but so far, hadn't tried to stop the custom. Probably there were other burglars, masked and carrying lights among the throng – it was set to be a lawless night. Livvy had never been out like this, in the middle of all the noise and excitement. When she was smaller, there had been trips to the pantomime, or the ballet. But she'd always been driven there in a cab, and the cab had come to the theatre door to collect them.

People called out to her, and shook her hand as they passed. Lights shimmered and dazzled around them; the darkness beyond was thick and mysterious. She found she was enjoying herself, and wished they could stay longer among the crowds, Cai firmly holding her arm.

His mother had not been pleased to see them go out. 'I know you're up to something, you,' she'd hissed at Livvy. 'If they bring my son back on a stretcher, I'll kill you with my own hands, so help me.' Of course Livvy had assured her that they weren't up to anything; they were just out to have fun. But she knew Cai's mother didn't believe that.

They passed through the city centre, and into the quieter suburbs. People were enjoying themselves more sedately here, though they came across one or two *Mari Lwyd* processions winding drunkenly across the silent streets.

And then at last they were in her own street. She could see lights in the window of 'her' house, but they didn't try to go round the front now. Instead, Solstice revellers no more, they crept around the side streets until they'd reached the alleyway. There was a bright half-moon in the sky and Cai doused his lantern. They could see shapes, everything colourless and indistinct, but enough to find their way.

There was no sound from anywhere as they followed the passageway to Livvy's back garden, no birds, no cats, only the wind rustling in the black and leafless trees. An arc of stars spanned the sky – she could name some of them, Orion, The Plough, the North Star. Her father used to point them out to her and promised that one day he'd buy a telescope so they could see the craters of the moon.

Her boots sounded horribly loud on the cobbles. Cai was creeping like a cat ahead of her. 'Stop here,' she whispered as they came to the climbing place.

He turned and put a finger to his lips. 'I'll sort the dog out. It'll take a bit of time. Just stay quiet.'

And she saw him in the darkness feeling the wall for where the footholds were. Then he started to climb, slowly, silently, to the top. At the top of the wall, he leaned over and peered around him. He turned to Livvy and made a thumbs-up sign. Then, very gently, he began to rattle and scratch the slates at the top of the wall.

The rest happened very fast. There was a sudden noise

of bushes being parted and a burst of barking. The guard dog had found them. Then before the dog had really begun to get going, Cai took the drugged bait from his pocket, and tossed it into the garden. At once the barking stopped as the dog went to investigate. Cai waited a while, leaning over the wall, and then he dropped down again to the ground. 'Give it a few minutes to take effect,' he whispered, 'and then we'll go over.'

'Cai, are you sure you haven't hurt it?'

He put his finger to his lips. 'Shut it, girl, and trust me.'

The two pressed themselves against the wall. From the other side they could hear the sound of slavering and crunching, and then heavy, gasping breathing. Then it stopped. They waited a while longer in case anyone from the house had been alerted by the dog's burst of barking. But nothing happened. Most likely the servants were enjoying a happy drink in the kitchen and weren't too bothered about things going on at the end of the garden.

'Right,' said Cai, after a while. 'Now we go over.'

'I'll go first,' she said.

'OK. But take care.'

She climbed up the wall, thankful that she was wearing trousers. At the top, she looked down. In the murk, she could just about make out the serpentine of the path, against the darkness of the shrubs. And there too, was a big humped bundle that might have been a dog out cold . . .

Then she swung herself on to the top, as she had done so often before, and over, and dropped down, not quite as lightly as she'd meant, into a bed of soft dry compost. A few moments later and Cai stood beside her.

Now she traced her way along the winding path. She knew it well enough not to falter, though here and there a loose stone nearly tripped her up, or a springing bramble grazed her face.

And then at last, they were standing in front of Minerva in her niche. In the grainy grey half-light she could see that the ivy – black by moonlight – had encroached once more, climbing over and around Minerva's helmet, trailing across her severe nose. Livvy felt a pang of guilt that she hadn't kept her father's garden a bit tidier. But it meant that half-hidden, no-one would have singled Minerva out for a storehouse of secrets. She tugged and pulled at the ivy. It came off in great handfuls and she dropped it on the ground. She was taller than when she had stood there with her father. Then she'd had to peer up at the statue, but now she stood eye to eye with her.

'Right?' whispered Cai.

Livvy nodded. 'If you can just hold her and tip her backwards, I'll look inside.'

Cai put his arms around the stone head, and lifted it, tilting it against him, just as her father had done. Livvy thought she heard a light metallic rattle. Then she put her hand into the dark rough space, and felt around.

For a few seconds, she could feel nothing except the coarse surface of the stone. And then at last, her fingers closed over something that had fallen against the back of the statue and had caught in the stone rim. It was cold and light, a metal tube.

And now she held it in her hand. It seemed nothing, a light metal tube with a screwcap, for cigars.

Cai let out a long, low whistle. He'd probably only half-believed her. Her fingers trembling, she unscrewed the cap and felt inside. Yes, there was something there. A roll of thin paper. Such troubles over something so small. Was this what her father had died for?

But there was no time to be hanging around. 'We've got to get out of here,' she said. 'We'll read what it is later.'

Cai didn't answer, but nudged her in the direction of the wall they had climbed. The humped dog-shape didn't move. It was harder to climb up, because there were no loose stones on the inside, but Cai gave her a hand up, and somehow, gracelessly, she managed to scramble over.

Soon she stood in the alley, the metal tube in her pocket – thank goodness men's clothes had such capacious pockets – and Cai was beside her. Then they were retracing their steps, swiftly, silently, through the dark, quiet streets.

# 24

And then it was back through the same crowds, the same lights and noise, but it seemed to Livvy that the lights were faint and muzzy now, and the noise of the crowd had ebbed. She felt strangely conscious of herself and every move she made, as though she walked in slow motion. And all the time she thought of what she held in her pocket, of the still unknown information that had caused her father to be killed. The journey back to Cai's house took forever, and yet no time at all, in this strange frozen dimension.

She came back to reality as he opened the front door. The house was in darkness. Cai for his part appeared exhilarated, intoxicated almost. Perhaps to him this really was all a game. 'See,' he said. 'Told you it would be easy.'

And, yes, it had been. What she thought would be the hardest part of her quest so far, unimaginably hard, had in fact been smooth and easy. They had found what she was looking for. Her fingers closed over it.

Inside the house, Cai pushed her into the dark living room. The remains of a fire glowed faintly in the grate. 'They've all gone to bed, thank goodness,' he said. 'I'll light the lamp.'

The light from the oil lamp startled her, showing Cai against his dark and jagged shadow, moving like a puppet. For a moment she felt threatened by everything, even him. But he came and sat down by her, talking quietly and gently. 'Well? Aren't you going to see what's inside?'

But still she could not bring herself to open the metal tube.

'Cai,' she said, suddenly remembering something that had troubled her. 'That dog. You didn't really hurt him, did you?'

He gave a disbelieving snort. 'Oh, Miss Softy! I told you, it didn't hurt him, no.'

'But you killed him, didn't you? You told me you'd tranquillised him, but you killed him.'

He put an arm around her, more gently now. 'And if I hadn't, we'd never have got into that garden. Or we'd have been torn to death. Or the servants would have come running and called the Scum. Get real, Liv. You can't always be ladylike.'

'I'm sorry you had to kill it,' she said sulkily. 'It was only a dog.'

'It was a souped-up killing machine,' he said. 'Now are you going to open that thing, or shall I?'

Suddenly she didn't want to be the first one to see it. She handed him the metal tube. 'You do it.'

'Suit yourself. All right. Here goes.'

He unscrewed the tube and extracted the little roll of paper. 'It's probably just a laundry list after all . . . No . . .'

He flattened the little bit of paper and held it to the light. 'No, it's not a laundry list.'

'Then what?'

'It's just names.'

'Names? Eight of them?'

'Yes. How did you know eight?'

'Let me see.'

She took the paper, and shifted to stand in the lamplight. For a couple of seconds she could see the words only as black shapes crawling over the paper like demented insects.

She must have been quiet for a long time, for after a while, Cai nudged her. 'Well? Does it make any sense?'

'Yes. Yes it does.'

'And . . .?'

'Like you said. Eight names.'

Eight names, written on a piece of thin rough paper, hastily torn from a notebook – you could see the ragged edge at the top. A scribbled note, in unfamiliar, not very literate handwriting:

*Here you are, boss, just the names so far. I'll get back to you when I've got more.*

No signature, no initial.

160

*Hector Varro*
*Gordio Alban*
*Adrian Vassus*
*Gregory Flavian*
*Cyril Leon*
*Timon Rufus*
*Quentin Tully*
*Otho Scaurus*

Eight names. And all those deaths, her father's, Uncle Paul's, Max's, just because of those eight names?

And one in particular . . .

Her father had seen this name, too. She couldn't imagine what it must have meant to him.

'Livvy? Who are they? What does it mean?'

She jabbed Gregory Flavian's name with her finger. 'My uncle. He's not really my uncle but I called him that. My father's best friend. Max's father's best friend . . .'

'. . . And?'

'This is the conspiracy, Cai. The eight names.'

'And one of them's your dad's friend?'

'His best friend. Our friend. And I think he was one of the people who got my father killed. These other names – I recognise most of them. Look – Gordio Alban – he's the commander in charge of the Brigantian Legions, at Carlisle. And Vassus – he's commander of the Atrebates, at Dover. I've met him. They're all big, Cai, all important men in the army. The eight men who are going to manage this . . . this revolution.'

'So who found all this out?'

'I've no idea. My father must have had a source. But whoever he was, he never found anything else out for Dad, it seems.'

'Maybe he was killed too.'

'It's possible. If they found out about my dad, they could have found out about him. Or the other way round . . . Oh, Cai, it's horrible.'

'So now you've got the names, what are you going to do?'

Livvy hadn't really thought this far ahead, but it seemed to her that there was only one course of action she could take now. 'I've got to get this information to someone I can trust in my dad's old barracks, I guess.'

'Can you trust anyone?'

'Well, at least I know who I can't trust now . . . But I reckon the new commander at the barracks, Commander Cato, he's all right. He was a friend of Dad's. And he's not on the list.'

'How will you get to see him?'

'Well, if I can get to the barracks . . . a lot of men there worshipped my dad. He was a real hero to them; he rescued three of his men under fire. They don't forget that, soldiers. If I can get to the barracks, there'll be men who remember him, who know me. Someone who can make sure I get to see Commander Cato.'

'You trust soldiers more than I do, Liv, I must say.'

Well, there were reasons for that; she could see that. 'I could trust my dad's men, Cai, with my life.'

'Well, if you say so. But I don't really like it.'

'You have a better plan?'

'No, not really. But as long as you have that piece of paper with you, you're at risk . . .'

Suddenly she thought of something and sat up. 'But I don't have to have it with me! Cai, have you got a really safe hiding place somewhere?'

'Er . . . yes, I think so. Why?'

'Where is it? Somewhere that doesn't endanger your family?'

'Well . . . on the boat. My stupid dad stashed a load of drugs there one day. It's under a panel, in the hold of the boat. You can't see where to get at it unless you know. We had police searches, dogs, everything. It was insane – he'd have been hanged if they'd found out. Me too, probably. But they never did. I reckon your piece of paper will be OK there. But you'll need to have it with you, won't you?'

'I don't need the bit of paper.'

'Where will you have it?'

She tapped her head. 'In here, of course. I've got a good memory. I can learn just eight names, no problem. Then they'll be safe. We should keep the bit of paper somewhere, though, for proof.'

'I guess that's the best idea.'

'It is. Can I take a candle up to my bedroom? Then I can get them inside my head before I go to sleep.'

Perhaps she was simply too confident. But the following morning, as she set off into the cold, flat aftermath of the wild Solstice night, she felt more easy than she had been for some time. All she had to do now was to get inside her father's old barracks – and get to the Commander. She was untroubled by the thought of this. There were so many men there who loved her father – enough to shield her from the unknown ones who were working against her. She might have to explain herself, to plead her case and say why she was dressed as a boy, but she'd be able to pass through the guards and find a safe escort, she was sure of it.

It had been hard, though, saying goodbye to Cai this morning. They'd been so close, and now their paths went in different directions. He must go and stash the document safely. He'd promised to do this and she had no reason to doubt him. He'd kissed her goodbye – out of sight of his mother, of course, and patted her cropped hair. 'Little short-hair,' he said. 'I shall miss you when you turn into a girl again.'

'So will I,' she said. 'I quite like being a boy. Goodbye, Cai.'

'Goodbye, Glyn Howells. And good luck.'

And that was it. No tears, no dramas, for which she was glad.

The streets were strewn with litter – streamers and glittery tinsel, empty bottles and mounds of vomit. The party was over and everything was quiet and crestfallen.

She had to cut right across the city to reach the barracks, and that meant going through the city centre. In the main square, she looked around her, remembering Muscovy Square, and how more exciting it had been than this quiet provincial place. But there were quite a few people around this morning, to her surprise.

Then she saw why. In front of the old Basilica, its ancient stones cleaned and newly mortared, its red roof newly tiled, there was a stone podium. Here public announcements had always been made in the old days, and still were in theory, though now they all had wirelesses, there was less need. But news might still be passed on through the Public Announcers if it was important enough, and this morning, it seemed, an announcement was to be made.

She should have ignored it, of course; she should have gone straight to the Barracks. But it was so rare an occasion now, and she wanted to see it. Other people had the same idea and they came streaming from the quiet side streets towards the podium.

Then the Announcer, who'd been waiting with his guards – two Military Police in dress uniform – mounted the podium. The guards sounded the strange old-fashioned trumpet call that heralded an important announcement.

Yes, Livvy should have ignored it and carried on her way. But she was curious and made her way towards the crowd. No-one was looking at her, anyway. All eyes were on the Announcer.

The trumpet call finished, and the Announcer began his preamble. 'On behalf of the Senate and the People of Imperial Rome, you are requested to hear . . .'

'It's the Emperor,' someone whispered. 'Must be the Emperor.' Then everyone fell silent.

No-one paid any attention to her, except one small girl, clutching her mother's hand, bored to death with the Emperor, and intent, in the way of small children, on staring at the tall thin boy in brown pleb clothes behind her. Disconcerted, Livvy smiled at her, then stuck out her tongue. Then she forgot her as she listened to what was being said.

'It has been announced from the Palace that our beloved Emperor is at present suffering from a slight infection. He is under the best medical care and regular bulletins will be issued. At present there is no need for alarm, but . . .'

Yet everyone present knew what this meant. If not already dead, the Emperor was certainly dying, and the people were being prepared for it.

The crowd was building up around her now. Livvy felt suddenly anxious among so many people – she'd not intended to be trapped in a crowd.

The Announcer, having finished what he had to say,

prepared to leave with his retinue. The crowd shifted and shuffled, talking to each other in careful anxious whispers.

No-one took any notice of Livvy. Except the child who'd been staring continuously at her with solemn eyes. Who noticed what a whole crowd of adults hadn't spotted. Who suddenly announced, in crystalline tones that rose above the quiet hubbub: 'Look, Mummy. That boy. It's the girl in the pictures!'


## 25

Everything was bolted down – that was what she first noticed. A wooden table, and chair that you couldn't shift from its fixed spot. A narrow wooden bed, a stiff horsehair mattress covered by a duvet. Behind a curtain was a toilet and washbasin. The door was steel – no handle on her side of it, and a grille at eye-level, so she could be observed. The tiny porthole was covered with mesh, through which she could see the slurp of grey water, and the high banks of the canal slipping past.

One of the guards had slipped her a pack of cards and a fashion magazine. Food – stodgy, decent food – had been brought to her at the usual intervals, though she'd hardly been able to touch it. They were gruff, unyielding, but not ungentle. It was rather as if they saw her as some sort of unpredictable and exotic animal. Livvy guessed they'd been instructed to treat her with courtesy, and this didn't come easy to Military Police in charge of a prisoner.

For a prisoner she undoubtedly was. All very well to go over that moment in the square and wish it undone, but it was too late for that. If it hadn't been for the sharp-eyed child, she'd have got away with it – but too late to think that as well.

After the child had cried out, things had happened with appalling speed. Looking around in panic, she saw only people surrounding her, and another tide of people surging slowly forward, blocking off any escape, even if she'd tried to run. It was the Emperor they had come to hear about, but they served very well as a citizen's arrest posse until the arrival of the Military Police. They thought, of course, they were restoring a poor misguided girl to the bosom of her family, and there was no point trying to persuade them otherwise.

The police had marched her – again, not hurting her, but with no possibility of evasion – around the corner, into a little dark building that she realised was one of the many Military Police stations that dotted the city. She'd demanded – of course she'd demanded – to be taken to the army barracks, but no-one took any notice of this. 'Sorry, miss. We've been given our instructions regarding you,' was all one of them would say. This was commonplace to them – no doubt people were detained all the time in this way – people who disagreed with the way Rome managed its affairs.

Next followed a humiliating passage. She'd been shut up in a little room, and a great burly woman with red arms and bad breath had come in, instructed her to take her clothes off, and searched her – all over and intimately – to make sure there was nothing hidden about her person. The woman refused to talk to her except to issue commands.

Then she'd been wrapped in a blanket and taken off to have a shower, under the gimlet gaze of the woman. She was glad of the shower, though she didn't like doing it in such company. Then new clothes were brought to her, girl's clothes. There was a long green dress, clean, but faded with much institutional laundering, and a brown woollen cardigan. She'd tried to appear jaunty and defiant – 'Green is just not my colour! I don't want to wear these things!' But it probably came out in a brattish squeak. And anyway the woman wasn't going to be swayed by that.

An hour, maybe two, had passed, alone in the little room. Sometimes people came and went. She felt strange now, with the long skirts flapping around her ankles, her breasts unconfined from her tight vest (at last she had some proper female underwear, only none of it quite fitted).

Then, two big policemen had filled the door. It reminded her of that morning they'd taken her to Ishtar. 'Right, miss,' they said. 'Orders are through. Come this way, please.' As though it were a request and not a command.

Then she'd been bundled into the back of a carriage parked in a back yard – she hadn't glimpsed the street again, the carriage doors were closed, shutters pulled down, a driver clambered up in front, and flanked by the burly men, they drove through unseen streets.

When they finally stopped, it was at the canalside. A fast police steam launch waited, and she was bundled inside, down a narrow gangway and into the little cabin that she now occupied.

It must be London she was headed for. And someone had sent specific orders about her. This was weird. She thought they might have sent her back to Ishtar, or to a girls' detention centre in Wroxeter – she'd heard of such

168

places. Or the barracks, but it was as if they – whoever they were – had realised that she couldn't go back to the barracks because of her father's reputation there. She couldn't go home, of course; she had no home. Tony was too far away to be consulted – and her mother! Goodness knows what was happening to her mother.

But why London? Who would possibly want to see her in London? And she would have maybe two days' journey before she could find that out. She wondered what Cai was thinking now, what he'd done when she didn't return. She wanted him there, but she was glad that he wasn't. She hoped there was still nothing to connect her to him, even though they now knew of her boy's disguise. But – and it was not a nice thought – now they knew how she had disguised herself, they could make enquiries about her – and someone might very well make that connection.

The two days passed slowly, unpleasantly. She'd never been a prisoner before, and she hadn't realised how it would scramble up her head. She couldn't think straight, couldn't eat, couldn't sleep. And at the same time she was filled with an overwhelming tiredness and lethargy. Even the games of Patience she tried to play couldn't fix her attention. It was as though she were listening to music all jumbled up, or trying to unscramble out-of-focus images seen from a fast-moving vehicle. Nothing would stay still inside her head for a moment.

But eventually – she could see through the little porthole that it was night – the little boat arrived at its docking bay.

And once more, the burly men came and took her out, holding her fast by the arms. Up the steps, out onto the deck, and with barely time to glimpse lights

169

shivering in watery reflections, down a gangplank, and into another horse-drawn carriage that had drawn up to the dockside.

Then, again, closed doors, curtained windows, guards flanking her, and a bumpy fast ride, the carriage twisting and lurching as they turned corners. And once again, no-one would talk to her. 'Best just be quiet, and wait and see, miss,' was all she could get out of her guards.

Then, perhaps half-an-hour later, with another lurch they came to a halt. The guards nodded to each other over her head, and one of them got down to open the door.

She scrambled out, blinking in the light of lanterns that were suddenly held up all around her. Her feet met smooth flagstones; she could see stone outbuildings, and behind her a large ornamental iron gate under a porticoed arch. There was a wall, windows, a porch with steps leading up. It looked like the stableyard of a smart town house.

The guards stayed with her, up the stairs, and into a tiled passageway. Riding boots were lined up along the wall, capes and jackets hung from pegs. It seemed vaguely familiar to Livvy but she couldn't quite place it.

Then through a door into a wide atrium. A small fountain plashed gently in the centre of white and black marble tiles, and palms and ficus trees flourished under a glass roof. Elaborate candelabra lined the walls, with electric lights that flooded everything in a bright shadowless glare. In the doorway, a few servants stood, dressed in formal London black. They looked curious but submissive, as though they had been told not to talk to the new arrival.

A wide staircase with marble balustrades curved up to a first floor. It was only when she stood on the bottom step that she realised where she was.

# 26

And so she knew exactly who would be waiting there, when the double doors were opened, and she was shown into a large, untidy semi-circular room, sofas and desk piled high with papers and books, wall niches filled with busts of sixteenth-century Italian poets. The tall man who had been standing behind the desk hurried to meet her, holding out his hands in greeting. He wore an open-necked collarless shirt, but a blue cravat with a bullhead pinned to it said as much as full dress uniform would have done about his profession. He was in his forties, the dark Roman eyes and hair, strong features, weatherbeaten skin. Gleaming white teeth showed in a welcoming smile.

'Livia, my dear, dear girl!' was what he said. 'We've been so worried about you!'

She took the hand that he held out, and he swept her into a formal hug.

'Good evening, Uncle Gregory,' said Livia.

'You look well, in spite of everything, I'm glad to say. Though . . .' he said, holding her at arm's length, 'taller when I last saw you – my dear girl, whatever possessed you to massacre your lovely hair like that? Well, sit down. You have a lot to tell me.'

She noticed that he sat in a chair, facing her across the desk like an interrogator. The guards had gone now, and he rang a bell to summon a servant. 'I expect you're thirsty,' he said.

She was – her mouth was dry as dead leaves – but she would have given the world to have been able to refuse the hot drink in an elegant crystal glass with a silver handle that soon was brought by a silent black-clad servant. She felt like Persephone about to taste the fruit of Hades. There was a decanter too from which Uncle Gregory poured wine for himself.

'Livia, dear,' said Gregory Flavian. 'Don't look so suspicious. It's just the spiced tea that Marcia makes for the girls when they come back from riding in the park. Talking of whom . . .' He nodded towards a gilt-framed photo of Aunt Priscilla and the daughters smiling at him from the desk. 'They will be very sorry to miss you, I'm sure. I sent them off ski-ing, just before the Solstice.'

The well-bred Livvy should have asked about their health, and sent her good wishes to them. But this was a new Livvy. She sipped her drink (hoping it wasn't drugged, but why should it be? Presumably they wanted her awake).

'Now, first of all, I want you to assure me that no harm came to you in your wanderings. Then I want you tell me just what it was you were thinking of.'

She swallowed hard. 'No, no harm came to me, thank you. Unless you count being frog-marched out of Forum Square by two thugs.'

'I hope they treated you well. Orders were to bring you to me if you were found. I didn't intend you to be roughed up.'

'I wasn't,' she said, staring him in the face. He took another sip of wine.

'All right, then. So the next thing to know is why? Why run away from a perfectly good school girls would kill to get to, dressed like a boy, sleeping Jove knows where . . .'

Livvy looked down at her drink again, and said nothing.

'Come on, Livia. I'm your friend, you know that.'

She should have kept quiet, but something sullen and argumentative inside her made her say, 'No, you're not.'

'Now, what is that supposed to mean exactly?'

Livvy, aware of the trap she had suddenly dug for herself, clamped her mouth shut.

'Livia, you can't just say something like that and expect me to ignore it.'

No, she couldn't. She looked up at him again, and said, 'Somebody was after me; that's why I ran away. And I think it was you.'

'No, why on earth should I be . . . after you? Unless,' and his tone changed, 'you know something more than you're saying.'

'I don't know anything. But . . .' and now it all tumbled out. 'Max was innocent, you know that. He didn't kill Commander Lucas, and you let him get killed.'

'Now, just one minute, Livia. Let's take this one step at a time. We all know what a lovely lad Max could be. We also know that he could be reckless. That's point one. Point two is that, yes, I don't believe he killed the Commander either, but he didn't give us a chance to prove anything to the contrary. Point three is that resisting arrest is never a smart thing to do. Guns don't know who people are, and soldiers are trained to make rapid decisions. I regret Max's death, deeply. But I must accept it as an inevitable accident.'

'Well, I don't accept it, I'm sorry.'

'I understand your anger, Livia. But you don't know the circumstances.'

'You wanted me dead, too!' she flared.

Gregory Flavian was silent for a few moments, as though he meditated on what she'd said.

'You see, that's where I don't understand you. You say you know nothing, and now you're giving me all sorts of bits of information that suggest that in fact you know a great deal. I imagine you're referring to that old secret police dossier?'

'Probably,' she said sulkily.

'Well, that was never going to be implemented. Not without my permission. But your family were in danger. Are in danger. I don't think you realise quite how ranks were closed to protect you.'

'Ishtar College, I presume.'

'Indeed. And a wonderful place, so I've heard, if you'd given it a chance.'

'And Tony?'

'Tony is on active service abroad. A secret location, which is why we can't broadcast it. I'm sure he'll be in touch when he can.'

'And my mother. Where have you dumped her?'

'Dumped, Livia?' he said in a pained voice. He reached over to take something out of a drawer, and handed it to her. A thick glossy brochure. *The Sanctuary Rest Home* it said in embossed gold letters, with a misty picture of a golden house amid trees. 'Just read this and tell me if you think we've *dumped* your mother.'

'No-one would tell me where she was.'

'Nobody kept anything from you. But they need to achieve some results with her treatment before she can have visitors.'

'And my house. Why does somebody else live there now?'

'Goodness, Livia, you are suspicious. A temporary arrangement. A legionary back from abroad and needing short-term accommodation while his own house is being

174

renovated. All arranged with your brother Tony before he left.'

It all sounded so sensible, so plausible. But there was something about it that told Livia that he wasn't telling the truth. She'd known a few convincing liars in her life, and they'd all lied like that, looking her straight in the eye, willing her to challenge them.

'Come on, Livia,' he said softly. 'Be straight with me, and I'll be straight with you. You aren't the innocent you make yourself out to be. You've been mixing with the wrong people, I know that for a fact.'

'Do you?'

'You and Max. I suspect were both flirting with terrorists. The Wolves or whatever they call themselves in their impossible language. What a pain they are, those West British. Always against everything.'

She snapped upright in her chair. 'The *Bleiddiaid* is what they're called. I know that much. But you're wrong. Max may have been involved with them, but I wasn't.'

'I do hope not, Livia. The people who left a bomb in a department store three years ago, who blew up a children's party at Colchester Barracks . . .'

'Shut up!' she flared. 'I'm not involved with them. And anyway, isn't what your people are doing just as bad?'

'*Our people,*' he said, very quietly. 'Now, I'm interested to know just what you mean by that.'

'You were one of the people who killed my father! You're on the list!' Well, she'd said more than she'd meant to now, but somehow it didn't matter. She had to confront Uncle Gregory – no, he couldn't be 'Uncle' Gregory any more – with what she suspected of him.

He was quiet for a long time. He poured himself

another glass of wine, and drank it, swilling it around the glass as though he were concentrating only on the taste of it.

'Very well, Livia,' he said eventually. 'You've put your cards on the table. I'm not going to ask you now how you've found out what you think you know. There'll be time for that later. But now let's have a talk about a few things, and maybe put you straight. After all, you want to survive all this, don't you?'

She didn't reply. Just drank the last few dregs of her spiced drink. It had grown cold now and the dregs were gritty with crushed cinnamon and nutmeg.

'The Empire,' he said, gently. 'Well, it seems strong, doesn't it? It's always been here, seems impossible that it won't always be. But it's a ruin, Livia, a sham, held together by heaven knows what. Our boundaries are shrinking, little by little. Other empires are rising to power, making the technological strides we should be making. If we survive the death of this Emperor, it'll be a miracle.

'And that's why we want to act. We want to restore the Rome of the ancient values, discipline, courage, morality, and we want to restore it in Britain. The other dominions, and New Rome itself, will eventually follow, we're confident of that. We want to establish a firm structure of government in which people can be free, really free in the best sense of the word.'

'We're free enough now,' she said.

'Oh, yes? So free that for years we've had to have a curfew? So free that children get blown up at their parties? Riots, strikes, drugs, street crime? What sort of freedom is that? Freedom comes from strength, Livia, strength and security.'

'And slavery, I suppose?'

'That's such an emotive term, isn't it? And yet enlightened slavery is the best way of protecting the poor; secure work for life, food, housing. Wouldn't most people regard that as luxury?'

'They'd regard it as slavery,' said Livia stubbornly.

'We'd call it *the bonded workforce*. There, that sounds better already, just with a change of word. There's nothing wrong with slavery, providing there are rules. I'm not talking about the old days of cruelty. A well-fed, contented slave has a security that a starving peasant just doesn't. He's part of one big family, a family in which everyone knows his place. And we want fewer rules, Livia, fewer, but stronger. Only we can't impose them in a weak system with everyone clamouring to have his say, or hers.'

'And women,' she said, 'what happens to us in this wonderful new world?'

'Oh, yes, I thought you'd come to that. Well, you're young, and full of idealism no doubt. But all the evidence shows that women are happiest doing what women do best, and that is keeping their home and family together. Why, I rely on Priss to keep me in one piece. Without her, I'm lost; my household doesn't function. We want women to have more respect, not less.'

'And what about sending girls off to be prostitutes? Ishtar girls?'

'My dear Livia, I don't quite know what distorted rubbish you've been hearing. You really should not listen to rumour. I told you, for *good* women, life will be only good. Bad women, like bad men, deserve what they get. And that's all I'll say on that matter. But what I'm

177

trying to persuade you is that life can only get better, not worse. And you can still be part of that better life, there's still time.'

'You killed my father,' she said stubbornly. 'I don't want any part of it.'

'Livia,' he said, and now his eyes were hard as onyx. 'I did not kill your father. I did not order him killed. But he was unwisely meddling in things he shouldn't have meddled with. I offered him the chance of becoming one of us, but he refused. If he'd just left it at that, he'd still be here now. But other people found out what he was up to, and took action. I couldn't stop them.'

'And Uncle Paul? I suppose you couldn't stop that either.'

'Paul Madoc committed suicide. A tragedy, but not the sort of tragedy you seem to have in mind. You're seeing conspiracy everywhere, silly girl.'

That's because it *is* everywhere, she thought but didn't say. She was feeling almost physically sick now.

'Livia,' he went on, looking at her intently. 'There's still a chance for you. Share your information with us, and you – and Tony – and your mother – will be safe whatever happens next. But I can only protect you for so long. Others know you're here and they'll grow impatient. Tell me what you know and who else knows it, or I'll have to pass you on to people who won't be so kind to you. You have tonight to think it over. Well. And also I have a surprise for you. An old friend who's longing to catch up with you.'

# 27

They'd put her in her old room, the one that she'd stayed in all those years ago. It was one of the old nurseries, right at the top of the house, so of course there were bars on the windows, and it had its own bathroom, so there was no need to leave the room at all. It was a pretty, girlie room, white wallpaper sprigged with delicate pink roses, pink bedspread scattered with lacy cushions, pictures of kittens and ponies on the wall. A long nightdress of fine embroidered cotton lawn had been laid out on the bed, with a couple of soft towels, and a towelling robe. On the dressing table, they'd left an array of lotions, face creams and scent.

The first thing Livvy had done was to make herself a hot, hot bath, with a good shake of expensive bathsalts. The scented steam rose around her and she tried to pretend she was relaxing. At any rate she was making the most of this brief interlude of luxury at someone else's expense. And when she'd finished, she wrapped herself in the bathrobe, and sat before the mirror, soothing face cream into her skin and manicuring her nails.

All around her, in the darkness beyond the barred window, London waited anxiously for the Emperor's death. No doubt there were guards at the porticoed gateway, bands of unruly soldiers roaming the streets, taking whatever caught their fancy, but up here, in all this soft pink-and-white tranquillity, it was hard to believe that any such things were going on.

But while she stroked cream into her face, Livvy was furiously thinking. The first thing she did was to run through the eight names again. She had tried to ensure a visual recall of the names on the piece of paper, and also, just for reinforcement, had made a mnemonic of the initials, techniques which had always worked well for her in the past. To her relief, the names were still embedded in her memory.

Then she considered her options. She had no doubt that this calm was only temporary, that soon, she'd be hauled off for some more stringent questioning. And the thing was, she really had no more to tell them. Her one secret was the names, and she'd already let that out. There was nothing else. Of course, with that information she was a danger and there was no question of her being released, but . . .

What worried her now was the trail she had left behind. She still had no reason to think that *they* – these still-hidden enemies – knew anything about her trip to London; only the *Bleiddiaid* had discovered that because they'd known who'd forged her papers. And she hoped that the canal community was a close-knit one, who wouldn't willingly help the police. She desperately hoped that she hadn't landed Cai and his family in danger. But sooner or later someone would spill the beans about the slim lad in brown who'd hitched a lift off the *Diligence* . . .

A knock at the door startled her. She hoped it was a servant bringing food – she was feeling hungry now, not having eaten properly for some days. A voice said, 'May I come in, Livia?' Then, without waiting for an answer, someone opened the door.

Livia scowled into her mirror, recognising her straight away. 'Oh, so you're the old friend who's longing to catch up with me.'

But there'd been a transformation. Lila now looked

merely tall, rather than big and gawky, and carried herself with confident dignity. Her mouse-brown hair had been styled and tinted a chestnut gold, and she wore a dress of soft printed wool, with an autumn pattern of tawny leaves. A chestnut-brown stole was flung over one shoulder, and she wore make-up and jewellery. The effect was elegant, fashionable – but also somehow, *middle-aged* – this new Lila was dressed in a way that was more suitable for someone's mother.

But she smiled with what seemed genuine warmth. 'May I?' She sat down anyway on a little chair covered in rose pink silk. 'I'm so glad you're safe.'

'No thanks to you,' said Livvy.

Lila sighed, and pushed back a gleaming strand of hair. 'You have to believe me, Livia, I wanted to be your friend. I truly, truly did. But duty always comes first, you know that.'

'Oh? And your duty included pushing people downstairs, and spying on them, did it?'

Lila put her face in her hands, but lightly, so as not, Livvy thought, to dislodge her make-up. 'Don't remind me of that. That was really horrible. But I had no choice.'

'Oh no?'

Lila looked up at her. *Oh, please help me just one more time, Livia dear! You're so clever!* 'I had no choice,' she said now, steadily. 'If you believed in something as I believe in this, you'd understand.'

'Oh, I believe in things,' said Livvy. 'But murder isn't among them. What are you doing here, anyway?'

'Ishtar became dangerous for me after you left. But my good friends – I have very good friends, Livvy – brought me here.'

181

'To the house of the man who killed my father. We all need friends like that.'

'He didn't kill your father,' Lila said softly, in a tone that made Livvy think of a cat facing a mouse, or a spider observing a fly. 'He was your father's friend. He's your friend, too.'

And something about the way her hand flew up to touch her hair made Livvy start. 'Oh,' she said, 'and he's *your* friend, too, is he?' Priscilla and the girls had been sent away. Why would Commander Flavian send them away in such dangerous times unless he had other games to play?

But Lila merely smiled enigmatically. 'The Commander is a wonderful man,' she said. 'A *wonderful* man.'

'You make me sick,' said Livvy.

'Livia, listen to me. You've got this all wrong.'

'Oh, have I? Then please do put me right.'

'Times are going to change, whether you like it or not. And you really don't want to be on the wrong side when that happens. It isn't too late. Just say the word and you can be part of all this. It's going to be wonderful.'

'So when you've finished killing all the people who don't agree with you, you'll be able to sit in your house, wearing all your fine jewellery, ordering your *slaves* about, and reflect on how wonderful everything is. Sounds great, Lila. I really envy you.'

'And what do you think'll happen to you? And your druggy mother? If you aren't with us, you're against us. Be on the right side, Livvy. It really is in your interests, I assure you . . .'

## 28

Another closed carriage, another rattling journey through unseen streets. This time, though, she knew where she was going. Lila had told her. They were taking her to the Mithras complex in the east city, the place she'd passed that morning weeks ago with Cai. Gregory Flavian hadn't shown his face again, for which she was grateful, presumably having left all to Lila's powers of persuasion. Which hadn't worked – whoever had thought Lila could move her had a bad sense of psychology.

But – and now it was starting to hit home – she was certainly no heroine, wouldn't be able to resist prolonged pressure. Even torture! Would they torture a fifteen-year-old girl? If only she knew a little more about what *they* were like. Sitting in the carriage, she began to run through her options. What she could tell them? No harm now in revealing her father's secret hiding place. And because she'd already said so much, she could say why she'd left Ishtar, could talk about her glimpse of the secret dossier. That was all, though, without implicating her friends. It was also all that she knew. But would they believe that? She tried to focus just on the moments ahead, to stop herself from the sickening thoughts that crowded in on her if she anticipated any further. She'd been so angry with Commander Flavian, that her anger had carried her through, all the time in his house, magnificently. Now all that anger had gone, leaving her feeling rather stupid. And in its place now had come fear, and fear wasn't magnificent at all.

Eventually, when the carriage lurched to a halt, and the door opened, she was taken out by two guards, one a wiry little man with dark hair, the other big and blonde, Germanic looking. Neither spoke to her, except to bark commands – 'this way, come along, turn right'. She had a quick glimpse of a courtyard surrounded by high walls, then she was pushed through a little door, along a corridor, down some stairs, along another corridor. No sound at all leaked through the heavy walls, but she could see a row of doorways stretching down the corridor. What was the temple doing with a prison anyway? Surely it was supposed to be a religious institution? Also she was female, and Mithras was supposed to be all-male. Things grew more confusing by the minute.

Then she was taken into a cell – again the bolt-down furniture, high barred window, and curtained-off lavatory. The smaller man said, 'You'll be processed tomorrow. Should warn you, it starts off nice and gets nastier, so if I were you I'd give in at the start. Well, you'll have the afternoon to think about it. I'll bring your supper at five.'

And then the door closed. After a while the noise outside died down. She tried rapping on the walls of her cell, but no answering raps came. So she sat on the hard bed, ran through her list of names, (still there!) and waited.

The hours passed. She tried to sleep, but couldn't. She wasn't tired anyway – she'd slept ridiculously well in her soft bed last night. The room was dark, with only a drizzle of light. In a wall-niche was a tiny candle stub, which would be her sole source of light later on. The walls of the cell were a sour sickly cream, and seemed to exude a bitter, nauseous smell, the smell, she thought, of fear, of all the people who had sat, without hope, in this confined place. The paintwork on the bed and table was scuffed and scored and worn down, gritty and sticky with dirt. There were scratches and marks on the walls, nothing she could read, but as though desperate fingernails had scrabbled there. Now it seemed to her that up to this point, she'd merely been playing games. It had been almost amusing, until now. She'd begun to feel that nothing could harm her, that she could outwit them all.

Now she saw how *stupid* she'd been. How, after all, they were cleverer than she was, and now they had got her trapped . . .

She pushed away thoughts of the future, and, to try to distract herself from the unthinkable, ran through her relationship with Cai, everything that had happened, right from the start. 'I wish we could get away from all this,' he'd said to her on the last morning before her rash trip to Forum Square. 'I wish we could just go somewhere and be together.'

'But where?' she said. 'You can't get away from Rome. Rome is everywhere.'

'Not true,' he said wistfully. 'My cousins have this farm in the West Cymric hills. It's great there, not like here. No papers, their own law . . .'

'If only,' she said.

'There are ways,' Cai had said doggedly. 'There are always ways.'

The time passed slowly, very slowly. If only the good parts of life passed as slowly as the bad! Her moments with Cai – that brief kiss, the conversations – they'd gone in a flash.

But then events took a sudden and unexpected turn. At five, the door opened, and the wiry man, carrying a tray, edged himself in. He shut the door behind him with his shoulder, put the tray down, and with a rapid movement had locked the door. She had time to wonder whether he intended to attack her. But instead he spoke in a rapid monotone.

'Look here, Livia Marcel, I've two minutes to say this, so shut up and listen. You'll have to think fast. We can get you out of here.' She opened her mouth to ask questions but he silenced her with a gesture. 'You met my colleagues a few days ago, I think. Been buying clothes in the market, hadn't you? Yes, thought so. We can get you out. But you'll have to give us something, information. We know you have it.'

'I haven't . . .' she said automatically. Then she tailed off. He was right; she had to think very fast. Suppose he was one of the *Bleiddiaid* sleepers the man mentioned as being hidden in the Mithras system? Suppose he wasn't? But he knew of the meeting in the east London square, which Gregory Flavian's people didn't seem to know about. Yet they were terrorists, or so people said. Should she give them information?

And what would happen if she didn't? Well, she had nothing to lose. 'I can give you the eight names of the chief men of the Order,' she said. 'That's all I know. But I do know that.'

An expression of surprise flickered briefly across his face. She could tell it was enough. 'Right then. This is what I'll do. You write the names down.' He took a stubby pencil and a notepad from his pocket and tore off a sheet. 'Don't let anyone see. I'll come back in half an hour to take your tray. Leave it under the plate. Then if we like what you've given us, I'll be back tomorrow at seven-thirty. Your escape will be set up – I'll explain it to you then.'

'How do I know I can trust you?'

'You don't,' he said briefly. 'But you can. Now is that a deal?'

'Yes,' she said, her head spinning. She had never made such an important choice so quickly in her life, she who could spend half an hour choosing between three shades of pink cardigan or two pairs of party shoes.

'Very well,' he said. 'I'll be back soon for that plate.'

# 29

A long night. A very long night. She thought she could hear someone moaning, the sound coming faintly and intermittently through the thick walls. Every half hour, a face peered through the little window in her cell door, making sure she hadn't escaped or killed herself, probably. She kept wanting to go to the toilet out of nervousness, and the little bit of food she'd eaten – some soup, a ham sandwich – was churning in her stomach as though she'd swallowed a banquet. She tried to keep her thoughts from wandering, but they would wander! Somewhere or other plumbing dripped and rumbled. Traffic rattled by in the street somewhere outside. A siren boomed distantly from the docks.

She didn't think she would sleep – but she did, a little, towards the end of the night, and woke up as the winter dawn began to be dispersed by winter light.

And then, it was seven-fifteen. She heard the rattle of a trolley in the corridor. Then her door was opened. The little man edged his way in.

'Right,' he said. 'We don't have much time. That was good stuff you gave us.'

'I'm glad.'

187

'You've got a good memory, remembering all that. And you'll need it. I'll say this once, quite quickly. You must memorise it as I go along, no second chance. Ready?'

She nodded.

'Right. At seven forty-five, they take you to wash and shower. Blokes take you, they let you go in the bathroom and shut the door. Not locked, shut, but they won't come in. There's a window there, barred. Pull at the bars – they're unscrewed. Open the window. Now, you aren't going out that way but you want them to think so. Turn the shower on full. Let it run.

'Just next to the shower, there's a panel covering a maintenance duct. Should be screwed in, but it's not. Pull it open. There's a passage inside, next to a pipe. You'll have to crawl. And it's dark. Hope you're not claustrophobic. When you're inside, pull the panel back into place behind you, just to conceal the fact that you've been there. It's easier to do than it sounds. They'll be looking through the window for you. It'll buy you a bit of time but not much – they'll soon work it out.

'Crawl along the tunnel, as far as it goes. Ignore the pipes and tunnels leading off. Eventually, the horizontal pipe joins a vertical pipe and the tunnel stops. There's a metal ladder going down a floor. Go down. In front of you, there's another panel, also unscrewed, conveniently. Now you're in a basement boiler room. Shouldn't be anyone there, but be careful, people use it occasionally. Go out through the door straight ahead. *Not* the door on the right, remember that. Takes you straight up a short flight of steps to a service door in the outside wall. Beyond that door, you're in the street; you're on your own then and we can't help you any more. Got that?'

188

Livvy nodded breathlessly. She had, she hoped she had.

He said, 'Good luck,' then he'd gone.

She passed the next few moments trying to go over and over what he'd said in her mind, making a map, visualising what she was supposed to go, so she could replay it, remembering all the steps. Girls weren't supposed to be good at this sort of thing.

They came at seven forty-five, just as he'd said. Two guards, new ones. They said, 'Livia Marcel?'

She nodded.

'You can use the bathroom. Shower if you want.'

She tried to look surprised. 'Great!' she said. 'I'd appreciate that.' But she didn't want to appear too jaunty or cocky. She took the threadbare towel from her washbasin and followed them to the end of the corridor. She could hear banging from some of the other cells as she passed.

At the door of the shower room, one of them said, 'Right. You have precisely fifteen minutes. After that, we come in, doesn't matter what you're up to, right?'

'I'll be ready,' she said, humbly.

The shower room was small, painted sickly green. There was a shower with a waterproof curtain, a toilet, a small washbasin. Of course, she'd formed a picture in her head of what the shower room was going to be like, when she'd been going over and over the plan last night. So it took her a valuable couple of seconds to adjust the mental image to the dimensions of the real room. There was the window, over the sink (she'd imagined it on the right). But the panel – just by the shower – was on the left, just as she'd pictured it, so that was a help.

The window was barred – it looked pretty firmly so. But as she gripped a bar, she found that it swung open like a door on hinges. The little window was a casement, and it opened silently, letting in a blast of December air, and showing a view of a courtyard, the back, she imagined.

Right. That was her decoy. She went to open the panel, then remembered that she hadn't switched the shower on, so she did that. She flushed the toilet too, just for good luck.

She had to loosen the wooden panel with her nails, but it soon came out. The screws had been removed. Beyond, she shuddered at a cobwebby black hole, a fat pipe going along it. She wriggled her head and shoulders into the hole alongside the pipe, and climbed in, pulling her skirts after her. Clearly it was intended as an access passage for repair workers, for though she couldn't stand upright, there was just about enough room to get through. Remembering what else the guard had told her, she put the panel back in place behind her. As he said, they'd soon work out which way she'd gone, but it would buy her a little time.

Now she was in the tunnel. The whole process had taken less than five minutes, so she had maybe another ten before they found she was gone. Moving on all fours, she made her way along the tunnel, cobwebs and dust brushing her face, her feet catching in her long skirt. It was dark, but she could feel the pipe beside her, and this helped her keep straight and move fast. Once, another pipe branched off, but she crawled over it, ignoring it, and went on straight ahead. She had no idea how long this went on – it seemed like forever, but was probably only a hundred yards or so.

Then, finally, she felt rather than saw that the horizontal pipe came to an end, now joining a vertical one. She could feel the edge of the floor. A small empty space opened before her, and there were the rungs of a metal ladder, just as he'd said. She turned herself round in the cramped space and lowered herself down backwards.

The ladder descended for perhaps the height of a room. Then another tiny cubbyhole, and another panel, through which the faintest chinks of light came. She felt the panel, trying to find a surface to give her purchase, and gripped the wooden framework at the sides. With a bit of pull and push, it started to move, and she inched it carefully away, looking all the time to make sure that there was no-one in the little room beyond.

A dingy little maintenance room, with a large noisy boiler taking up most of the space. There was also a table and a chair. The chair was pushed back, and there was a four-day-old newspaper and an empty tea-stained mug on the table. Opposite the boiler, on the right, was a door – that must be the one she'd been told not to take.

And in front of her was a door with a glass panel. She could see steps through the panel, steps leading up to freedom.


# 30

Instinctively, she did not rush across the room, but edged round it, her back to the wall. She paused to catch her breath in front of the door on the right, but kept her eyes on the other door, with its flight of upward-leading steps visible through the glass panel.

And then suddenly she saw something that made her already lurching heart drop like a stone. A boot appeared on the uppermost step, became an ankle and a leg, and was followed by another boot.

Luckily – if anything could be said to be lucky in these circumstances – the person was coming down quite slowly, so she grabbed the handle of the other door – the wrong door. She prayed that it was not locked, and turned it.

It was open. She opened the door just enough to admit her, and had slipped through the gap and closed it behind her, all in a few seconds, hoping she had moved quickly enough not to be seen.

Now she must try and find another way out.

It was a long, dim corridor, lit only through occasional shafts of light from slits in the roof; it must be deep in the basement.

The corridor went straight for a while, then turned right. It was getting darker now, and the light shafts fewer. Then abruptly it branched in two. 'Left or right, Minerva?' she said, asking the goddess who seemed to have been kind to her in the past. Left, Minerva seemed to say, so Livia turned left. Up above, they must be looking for her by now. She wondered what they were doing, how many of them there were, and how long it would take them to realise that she hadn't left through that open window.

This corridor went on in a descending curve, so that she had no idea which direction she faced. Maybe Minerva had misled her. It was quite dark now, but she could just about make out the walls. It all smelled damp and musty.

The corridor terminated suddenly in a short flight of steps that she almost tumbled down, and then a door. The door opened, and she went through.

The musty smell was stronger now, and reminded her of something. It felt icy cold, and now the walls were rough. There was a prickling acidic tang to the air, and she tried to recollect where she'd smelled it before.

Her hands moved over the walls – rough stone – and then she realised – old buildings! This was exactly like the smell of archaeological excavations she'd been taken to – the baths at Chester, the northern Governor's villa at York; ancient stone and lime mortar, earth and the damp of centuries. She must now be in the oldest part of the complex, maybe the Mithraeum itself.

The stone corridor went on – less directly than its modern counterpart. It curved, it sloped down, it went through an arch over rough ground, it emerged again, and seemed to wind back on itself.

And then it opened out to a wide dim hallway. There were little niches in the walls, lit by the flicker of tiny long-life candles. They'd burn unattended, slowly and faintly for days at a time. The walls were plastered, with remnants of ancient decorations in that pink the old Romans loved, peeling away. She saw myrtle leaves, and vines, twining and twisting. Numerous archways off this corridor led to little dark rooms; here and there a painted face stared out imperiously at her from the gloom, or a painted hand clutched a knife. The silence was complete, the silence of deep underground, surrounded by stone and earth, a dead silence without echoes, a silence in which you could scream and no-one would hear. Livvy shivered, and not from the cold.

The corridor bellied out around a dark archway, larger than the others, of carved stone, the patterns worn and muffled. A few branches of leaves – dried up and dusty now – had been laid out at the foot of the wall, and a wreath of dusty dead foliage hung at eye level, tributes from some long-ago ceremony.

It was only a small room, with a vaulted ceiling that made it like a cave, lit by a drizzle of faint light from above. Stone benches surrounded the walls, which ended in a semi-circular bay. Somehow, the very smallness of the temple sanctum, the compaction of so much ritual, so much faith, made it more chilling than a larger space would have been. The silence seemed to thicken and curdle – there was an air, somehow of accumulated *fear,* though there was nothing ostensibly fearsome about the ancient stone altar that stood there, with the old soldiers' god, Mithras, in his Persian cap and short cloak, a sword raised elegantly in his hand, a bull prone before him.

He was a figure familiar from army shrines, but she had never seen him so hidden and buried and secret as he was here in this underground place. All those thousands of years of secret, sacred ceremonies. She felt surrounded by invisible malign eyes, silent voices, the spirits of men who'd stood here over the years, performing their hidden rites and ceremonies, and her stomach tightened with just the sort of superstitious fear her father had taught her to despise. Even if you didn't believe in them, ghosts could strike you cold.

Here was the ancient Mithraeum, the most sacred place in Britain for these people, and one where she had absolutely no right to be at all – both as a girl, and as a civilian. It was here that men would come, tracing a ceremonial route through all the little rooms beyond, each with its element of ritual, to reach this holy of holies, as they had done for hundreds, thousands of years. She and Max had often tried to guess what happened then, joked about it, even: was there blood?

Did they *drink* it? Did they sacrifice things? Animals, *babies?* Did they eat babies? At which point in the conversation, Max would pretend to be slavering over an infant limb, and Livvy would collapse in giggles. It had all been quite funny then, in the sunlight and open air. (Oh, Max!)

At any rate, initiates were supposed to be reborn, reborn and renewed. But she could hear her father's angry murmur – *Mumbo-jumbo, Liv – all mumbo jumbo!*

And the initiates of Theta – that last, extra, murderous mutation of the cult – they too must have come here and made their poisonous vows.

She'd wanted to smile now, but she couldn't. If any soldier ever found out – ever – that she'd been here, contaminating the sacred stones, he'd kill her, for sure. She couldn't tell anyone. Except perhaps Cai, one day. (Oh, Cai!)

For a few moments she stood there, listening to the sound of her breathing. As though all that ancient fear had paralysed her. Then she took a grip on herself, and forced herself out of that horrible, tainted place.

She hurried along the rest of the corridor, leaving those little arched doorways still holding their secrets. Her feet thudded on the old floor of hard piled earth.

Then the corridor twisted again, and began its wanderings. Up, along, round and about, only just wide enough for her to squeeze through in places. Up another flight of worn stairs.

And then at last, she came to a door, a flat, modern door on a steel hinge. She pushed it open, into a blast of normal modern air, and a modern cream-painted corridor. As she shut the door behind her, she saw a notice in large letters:

195

## STRICTLY NO ENTRY
## AUTHORISED PERSONNEL ONLY

And now she was back in her own century, a basement corridor – for it still seemed that she was underground – lit expensively by bowls of electric light in the ceiling, seemingly purposeless.

But it had a purpose, for suddenly it split into two, and a painted sign with an arrow indicated 'Maintenance Only'.

The door of the first room in the maintenance corridor was half open. There were lockers along one side of the wall, wooden chairs, and a row of pegs. On the pegs, someone had hung a workman's blue overall and a blue peaked cap.

Livvy's hand flew to her short boy's hair. Could she? Could she get away with it again? She picked up the overall and held it against her. It was stiff and heavy, almost like holding up a person. And it seemed to have been made for a youngish, smallish man. 'Minerva,' she said aloud, 'don't let anyone come in, please.'

Quickly she whipped off the hated green dress and the horrible brown cardigan. She undid the buttons down the front of the overall and stepped into it. The trousers and sleeves were both a little long, but she turned them up. The long trousers might hide the light girls' shoes she still wore. Then she pulled the peaked cap down over her face, and smiled to herself. Glyn Howells had just got himself a job as a janitor. The dress and cardigan she rolled up and stuffed into a corner, wondering what the workmen would think when they came across them.

A long stiff bristle bush leaned against the wall, and

196

she picked it up. Now it was back to the corridor, and continuing by a way she'd not taken before. She couldn't believe that she hadn't passed anyone – where had everyone gone? Still, she'd been lucky so far, and she could only pray for such luck to continue.

There was a flight of steps, dingy back stairs, leading up, and she followed them. At the top was a double set of glass doors, and suddenly she could hear voices and see people moving.

She pushed open the doors with her shoulder and came out, casually, as she'd seen workmen do, head down, broom in hand. Through lowered lids she saw that now she was in a smart part of the temple complex – a floor of green and white mosaic, beautifully done, white-painted walls, pillars, the flood of light everywhere. A wide entrance hall – and she could see a big revolving door that must – surely – lead out to freedom.

Who were all these people? Men, of course, all men, in army uniform, though many of them hadn't put on their jackets, as though they'd come in a hurry. They came swarming downstairs, pushing through swinging doors, gathering in anxious clusters. From an open doorway came the sound of a radio, and another. Slow sonorous music was being played. Then she heard in the distance the sound of a bell being rung – a steady clang, clang, clang.

At first she thought they were all looking for her – the escaped prisoner. Then she saw the intensity with which they were talking, their concentration, taking no notice of anything around them. She edged closer and closer to the main doors.

Four big men stood by the doors, heads down. And she noticed that one was wiping tears from his eyes. But

197

another was angry. 'Today of all days! How did we let it happen?'

The revolving door spun, round and round and round. And with every spin, more men surged through, coming from outside into the building. They were anxious, breathless, excited.

She saw a gap in the revolving door, although it was spinning fast, and managed to slip into it, to be disgorged on the main steps of the building a few seconds later. Men still swarmed up the step. It seemed everyone wanted to get in – only she was trying to get out.

She recognised now where she was – she'd stood beyond those gates with Cai. She looked around her at the wide courtyard and the dark jumble of the old city beyond, then she propped the broom against a pillar, and marched firmly off, down the steps and into the courtyard, against the flow. And no-one stopped her.

# 31

The gate was shut, with two soldiers guarding it. They were letting men through in ones and twos.

'Where you going?'

Livy kept her cool. She said, gruffly, 'Home. My shift's finished.'

'Oh, your shift's finished; that's all you lot think about.'

A man coming to the gate gripped the fancy iron work tightly. 'Is it true?' he called across Livvy's reluctant conversation.

'It's true.'

'And the other business?'

'That too. Get in quick.'

And as he opened the gate to admit the other man, Livvy slipped out.

As she rounded the corner, she began to see why people were so anxious to be inside. A gang of men, about a dozen, held bricks and torn-out posts. Bricks were being thrown at anyone unwise enough to get in their way. For the moment, the armed guards were inside the gates, letting people in, but any time now, they'd be outside, and things would get nasty. Livvy held up her hands as she approached the mob. 'Let me through,' she said. 'I'm not one of them.' Though she had no idea which was the right side to be on, or who anybody was. Just better to be out of the way.

The man with a brick lowered it and waved her on. Maybe he wanted Roman soldiers, not workmen. 'Get out!' he said. 'Go!'

She dived into a silent street between dark warehouses, up a narrow passage, past a boarded-up bathhouse and a row of little houses ready for demolition. It seemed unnaturally silent. But then she came out into one of the city streets, a dark line of banks and law firms and offices. People had poured out of the office buildings and stood bemusedly around on the steps, as if they had been washed up there by a flood. She heard someone say, 'When?' and another answered, 'About twenty minutes ago, the news came.'

A bell started pealing from a city temple, just as she had heard before, a slow solemn clang. 'The Emperor!' she thought. 'It must be the Emperor.' She could only thank the late Emperor for providing so convenient a distraction.

She was still in danger here, so close to the Mithras temple. Amid all the confusion, someone might still be searching the streets for the fugitive prisoner with dangerous information. Her only chance was to try and get to the Senate and persuade someone to let her see the Governor. And the Senate was a good half hour away, in the West End.

That way lay the eastern suburbs, where she'd been with Miss Lena. Over there was where the trams terminated. But down the road was Fleetgate, where one of the old city gates had stood, and whose ruins could still be seen, among manicured banks of earth, carefully preserved as an archaeological site amid office blocks. There used to be a river here, running down to the Thames, but it was covered over now, and a narrow street of temples and law courts ran down in the eventual direction of Muscovy Square and the Senate.

At the corner of Fleet Street was a tobacconist's; from the doorway a large man with a beard and red face was expounding his opinions to anyone who'd listen. Little groups formed and dispersed around him and went their separate ways. Nobody seemed much upset by anything that had happened; everyone was excited and keyed up.

'. . . Worse before they get better, you mark my words!' the bearded man called out to a couple of women with headscarves and shopping baskets. Livvy recognised someone who loved the sound of his own voice and decided to make the most of it.

'Excuse me,' she said in her normal voice, rapidly dropping an octave when she remembered. 'Can you tell me what's happening?'

If the man was disappointed to have only one young lad in working overalls as audience, he didn't show it.

'Well, lad, where to start? If you ask me, things'll get a lot worse before they get better, believe me.'

'Is it the Emperor?'

'Oh, it's the Emperor all right.'

'What happened?'

'Well, let me see, I'd just opened up, and I'd put on the radio as I usually do, and I must say the news was pretty shocking, I thought. But then I thought, well, let's just hear the weather forecast and then make my tea which I always do before the hordes come. But then blow me if they didn't interrupt the weather forecast, with the news about the Emperor. Put the other stuff right out of my mind, I can tell you.'

'So the Emperor's dead?'

'So they say.'

'How dreadful,' said Livvy politely. You had to be careful what you said in public.

'Eight o'clock this morning they released the news. Said he'd – whatever they call it – breathed his last at seven-thirty, though it's my guess he went long before that and they just saved it up for the morning bulletin. Of course I can't say I was surprised, not like I was by the other stuff.'

'What other stuff?' asked Livvy. But if she'd hoped for a straight answer from Mr Beard, she was disappointed.

'Well, lad, that's why I say it'll get worse before it gets better. It can't just be coincidence, can it? There's something going on, believe me.'

'So what did happen?'

'Well, these assassinations. Say it's a coincidence, and I'll say you need your head examined.'

'What assassinations?'

'Well, this morning, in his carriage, six o' clock, stopped at a traffic light, machine-gunned down. That bloke always in charge of Memorial Day, impressive, I thought. Flavian, he was, Gordo, Gregory, whatever his name was . . .'

'Commander Flavian is *dead?*'

And two other chaps, one in Silchester. Ver . . . Vor . . .'

'Varro. Hector Varro?'

'Yes, Varro, that's the fellow. And another one in . . . York, I think.'

'Tully? Rufus? Scaurus?' asked Livvy softly.

' Scaurus. Odd name . . . Can I help you, madam?'

A woman had come up. 'Well, I just wanted some cigarettes. But they're saying the Emperor . . . the Emperor's dead?'

And he turned the beam of his attention on her, delighted to have another chance to tell his story. 'Well, I'd switched my radio on, just to get the weather forecast . . .'

Uncle Gregory.

Uncle Gregory, sitting smiling in his chair, and now dead.

Well, the bearded man had been right about one thing. No, it couldn't have been a coincidence.

*I did that*, thought Livvy, remembering the bit of paper she'd left under her plate last night. *I did that. I killed him . . .*

Dazed, she barely noticed what was going on around her, as she went down Fleet Street. He'd been her enemy, and her father's enemy, but she'd not imagined him – or wanted him – dead. They must have moved fast, the *Bleiddiaid*, must have had their killer squads ready and waiting for a signal, knowing as everyone had guessed, that things were going to be chaotic when the Emperor died.

The death of the Emperor. That surely must be what *they* – the members of Theta – were waiting for, too. The deaths of three of the eight would surely cause some confusion and maybe delay to their plans, but probably wouldn't be enough to stop them. In spite of everything, she thought, she must get to the Governor as soon as possible with her information. The army would know how to deal with Theta. It had to be destroyed; she owed it to her father to do all she could to further that aim, even if her feelings about the army had changed.

She had reached Muscovy Square now. Victory's gold paint was muted in the dull light. She remembered how she had last seen the Square, the shops full of Solstice decorations, people excited and happy – in spite of the dangers that lay in wait for them after dark. Now the shops looked empty and bleak. Some shopkeepers had already got the black wreaths up in their windows and the swathes of black crêpe paper – must have stockpiled them, ready for the news.

One or two people – elderly women mainly – were tearful, but Livvy noticed that most seemed indifferent. Maybe they feared what would come next, for surely everyone could sense revolution of one kind or another in the air, and no-one could feel enthusiastic about the Emperor's probable successor, his playboy grandson Gaius.

Beyond Muscovy Square, through the Victory Arch, stretched the long straight Julian Avenue, down to the Senate and the Governor's Palace. Last time she'd been there, it had been in an open carriage, her mother wearing a gorgeous hat piled with roses, her father immaculate in his dress uniform, on their way to receive his medal. Now she was a strange-looking young man in a blue workman's uniform, one among a crowd.

As she looked down the Avenue, she could see the end of a column of men in uniform, marching towards the Palace. 'What's happening?' she asked the man standing next to her.

Everybody had his theory today. The man said, 'Oh, they've been moving troops in all week. I reckon they've known about this for ages. Anticipating trouble, if you ask me.'

She made her way across the wide road, darting between carriages, and under the Arch. Then down Julian Avenue, along which everyone else seemed to be hurrying too. The column of soldiers came to a halt in front of the Senate, wheeled sharply round, and started filing into the courtyard. As she watched, another column of men came through the park, and turned into the wide avenue. She saw the flash of their red berets, and the faded blue of their uniforms . . .

The Thirteenth Cornovians. Her father's old regiment.

She ran, and soon caught up with the column. It was a smallish detachment, about fifty legionnaires, a century-captain at either end. They were marching in strict order, heads held high, looking straight ahead, the ruthless, disciplined backbone of the Empire, the fighting machine that had kept everything together for so many centuries.

And she recognised one or two faces among them. Men who would know who she was, men who had loved her father. She drew abreast with them, and then ran alongside them, breathlessly, like a silly camp-follower.

They did not turn their heads to look at her, though she sensed that they were aware of her, and would move fast if she became a nuisance.

She called out to them. 'You have to help me! I'm not a boy! I'm Livia Marcel! I'm the daughter of Felix Marcel! You must help me! I have to see the Governor.'

Eyes had flickered left, taking her in. 'Please,' she called again. 'Captain Marcel! You know me! Please. Something terrible is going to happen!'

And then, almost silently and almost as though it was part of their routine, two men slipped sideways, out of rank, moved either side of her, and were joined by the captain at the tail of the column who also slipped out of rank. She found herself now incorporated back in the marching column, keeping up with them. The head movement was imperceptible, but they were looking at her now. 'You have to help me!' she implored. 'I have to see the Governor! My father had information! I have to tell him. Please.'

And then, for the first time in this whole business, suddenly and shamefully and girlishly, she burst into tears.


# 32


From her vantage point, leaning out of the window, she could see that the cherry trees lining the road were already starting to come into blossom, and the street would soon be heaped with billows of pink. There'd be hyacinths and narcissi, too; she imagined them suddenly poking their heads out of the dark corners of her father's garden, making little pools of clean, pure colour among the dead leaves.

Everything looked very peaceful from here, as the red roofs swept down towards the city centre. She could just about see the towers of the barracks, and in the other direction, the golden spire and dome of the big Jupiter temple. But it wasn't peaceful, though. Bursts of rioting had been going on for weeks after the Emperor's death, quickly suppressed, but springing up again. Bombs had been left at coach stations and stores, though so far there'd only been one bombing attempt here in Wroxeter, and no-one had been hurt. The main force of the army now had to be concentrated on the serious split that had happened in the south at Dover – the mutiny of an entire garrison under the leadership of Adrian Vassus. All over the country, legionnaires were deserting, making their way to the south to join the mutineers, Theta sympathisers now coming out of the woodwork, the ghost army that until now had moved unseen. The mutiny was being suppressed with Rome's usual brutality, captured mutineers being summarily shot with only the briefest of court-martials. But it hadn't been suppressed yet, not by a long way.

However, it had helped that they'd known who the ring-leaders were and had been able to act quickly. Of course, Flavian, Scaurus and Varro were already dead – the *Bleiddiaid* were suspected, though no-one knew quite how they had got such good information ahead of the government. Tully and Rufus had been arrested, though Gordio Alban and Cyril Leon had vanished – it was believed that they'd fled abroad, perhaps to Iberian Spain, a province known for its more extreme Mithraic cults. Investigations were now going on into the activities of the men, and so far Livvy had heard nothing. It was unlikely of course that she would ever know the whole story. The military would only release such information as they wanted; the rest would be indefinitely locked up in some secret archive. The bulletins issued in the official government newspapers stressed that the rifts were only temporary and order would be restored soon.

But even Livvy, cut off as she was, could sense that things were different now, different and dangerous. No-one could summon up much enthusiasm for the new Emperor Gaius, with his string of smart carriages and racehorses and his taste for pretty actresses. And a new kind of political movement seemed to be happening: strikes that weren't simply about more money, riots that weren't just about destroying shop windows, but with demands for other things – like democracy, like votes for everyone, like citizens' rights, like civilian rule – like a *Republic* . . . How strange it all was.

Yet, the bearded man in Fleet Street had been right – things would get worse before they got better – the military weren't going to cede any ground without a struggle. No wonder Livvy wasn't being allowed out much these days.

She had been made a temporary ward of the commander of her father's old regiment and his wife – Commander Cato, and his wife Diana. The Catos were a middle-aged couple, parents of three grown-up sons. And Diana Cato didn't at all like girls. Livvy had overheard her muttering one day to Iris: 'So *sneaky* and spiteful. I just think boys are . . . you know . . . so much more straightforward and honest, don't you?'

Iris of course had agreed, even though she'd been

landed with the unwelcome task of being Livvy's chaperone. She'd been nurse to the straightforward and honest boys and considered it very beneath her dignity to be landed with this little slip of a thing from a dubious family of inferior rank.

But here Livvy would have to stay until things were sorted out. Of course, they were being sorted out – her lawyer, who was supposed to be representing her interests, assured her that everything was being done. And it seemed that the army was prepared to dip into its copious funds to protect a girl whom they still saw as one of their own. For investigations had revealed that there had indeed been a plot to undermine, if not destroy, the Marcel family. Livvy had now been taken to see her mother in the rest home – she had been stuffed full of powerful sedatives. The doctor in charge of the Home had been dismissed, though no-one could quite pin down who was to blame. But her medication had been changed, and she was gradually being nursed back to health. Livvy had hardly recognised the pale and distraught figure propped in a high hospital chair. Her mother had barely recognised her either. All Livvy could do now was hope that her mother hadn't been permanently damaged by the treatment – time alone would tell. Probably everything would be hushed up, and she'd never find out what had really happened.

The new tenant of her house was a reality. As Uncle Gregory had said, he was a returned legionnaire, and though he'd been used as part of someone else's intrigues, and no, Tony had not been consulted, the tenant himself was apparently innocent of devious conduct. It had been decided – not by Livvy, who wasn't consulted either – that he and his family would be allowed to see out their tenancy, which would be over in a couple of months anyway when his new house was ready. They'd even offered to let Livvy visit, to make sure they were looking after the house, but she couldn't bear to see it in different hands, with strange servants. Everything would be just the same when she went back home with Tony and her mother, they assured her, but she knew it couldn't be. For one thing the servants had all moved to different positions – they probably wouldn't be able or maybe even want to return Everything must be different now.

Tony, who had so far survived his dangerous posting abroad, would not be home for some weeks. Letters arrived from him to Livvy, in his usual tone. Yes, indeed she'd had a difficult time, but surely she could have gone to the authorities before, rather than prancing about all over the country in disguise and putting herself and the family reputation so horribly at risk . . . Well, thank you too, Tony. Really looking forward to seeing you.

And there was Cai. Through a campaign of sustained and persistent nagging, she'd managed to persuade Mrs Cato to let her have a meeting with Cai. But it had hardly been a success. Letters had passed to and fro, and eventually a meeting had been set up in the café of Astra's department store, a place for old ladies and little girls out of ballet classes, a place that had put Cai at a disadvantage from the start.

Diana Cato had placed herself a few tables away, and toyed with her low-fat chicken salad, while Livvy, in a new outfit of dark red wool and a purplish scarf – her choice of colours – but Mrs Cato had chosen the old-fashioned, dowdy style – faced an uncomfortable Cai across the table. At every attempt he made to take her hand, Mrs Cato had coughed not very discreetly and raised plucked eyebrows disapprovingly. 'I can't be doing with this,' Cai had muttered angrily, and she'd tried to tell him not to mind, she couldn't help it at the moment, but she'd find some way to meet him properly. She had so much to tell him, but had been able to say so little of it, as he sat stiffly before her, under Mrs Cato's hard stare. In the end she said, 'I'm sorry, Cai. I'll try and get out of this. I really will. I'll find a way.' And he'd managed a faint lopsided grin, the shadow of his usual smile. 'You'd better, Glyn Howells. I'm not coming here again.'

She tried writing to him but, as Mrs Cato insisted on seeing all her letters, it was almost better not to write than have to be censored. He'd come to the house one day too, but all she heard about it was when Iris hissed at her some time later, 'That scruffy young man of yours tried to get in the other day. The cheek of it! Madam soon sent him packing, I can tell you.' She'd managed to write a brief note to Miss Lena (also not approved of in the Cato household) but could say very little other than that she was safe and thanking her for her hospitality.

One dreadful thing had happened, though, and it was partly her fault. In the course of the routine investigations into her disappearance, the Military Police had visited Don, her old teacher. It had been a Saturday, and they'd found him drunk. There'd been an enquiry; several anxious parents who'd always suspected him, and one or two ex-pupils who were never happy at Sixth Precinct had come forward. And now he'd been suspended, and Sixth Precinct was closed. Under considerable protest, Mrs Cato had let her write a note to Don saying how sorry she was, and also under considerable protest, she'd been allowed to read his reply, which came a few days later.

'Don't blame yourself, lassie,' it read. 'I've been living on borrowed time and they were always going to catch up with me some day. I'll probably go back to Caledonia and maybe write that book at last, if I can stay sober long enough. I'll miss you girls, though – all that sparkle and brightness. And though I'd never have said it to your face, you were one of the brightest of the bunch. Don't waste that cleverness, mind. Don't drown yourself in ladylike hobbies. I expect great things of you . . .'

Diana Cato had read the letter first, and tutted as she handed it to Livvy. 'And to think this man was in charge of a girls' school!' Arrangements were now being made to send Livvy to one of the conventional girls' schools in the city – no question of her going back to Ishtar, of course (now also under investigation) but this place probably wouldn't be much better in terms of education. It seemed that all of Livvy's prospects, having opened up briefly, were now closing in on her again. Whichever way she looked, she saw prison.

Sometimes she felt she should have got a little more credit for what she had done – but of course things didn't quite work out that way. She didn't get to see the Governor, of course – probably that would never have happened. But she'd been treated well in the main barracks where she'd ended up, been given food and proper clothing. Though she'd been searched for weapons, it wasn't the humiliating body search she'd had at Wroxeter. Then she'd been taken in front of three senior investigating officers.

She'd wondered at first whether she could trust them. Anyway, she'd risked it, and told them everything. Or nearly everything, anyway. She didn't tell them about Cai, and she didn't tell them about the *Bleiddiaid*. And she certainly didn't tell them how she'd traded information for freedom. No-one was going to find out about that, except perhaps Cai, one day.

It turned out that there had been strong suspicions about the Order of Theta and the activities that went on under the name of Mithras. Some of the men on the list had been suspected for some time, but nothing could be proved against them. Not that her father's anonymous list could count as conclusive proof, but it certainly provided enough evidence to make further enquiries. (The actual list, as far as she knew, was still hidden in Cai's boat, but it was useless now, having yielded up its secrets.) The mutiny at Dover showed beyond doubt that a revolution had been planned to take place on the death of the Emperor.

She was also interested to find out that indeed Mithras had no authority to imprison, and that was to be investigated straightaway. She hoped those unseen fellow occupants of the cells would soon be freed. There was much about the Mithras Complex, the Sol Invicta Centre, that needed looking into, and Livvy was sorry that she would probably never know the true story. What had happened to Lila she never found out, either. She vanished into one of the holes of history. Nor did Livvy know what happened to Gregory Flavian's family. She didn't imagine they'd ever want to speak to her again. And as for Max – well, though people seemed willing enough to believe that maybe he wasn't the murderer of Commander Lucas, no-one was eager to stir all that up again. The Commander would be unavenged, and Max would not be exonerated. That was how Rome worked.

The officers had treated her courteously, but even they seemed to think that she'd rather stepped out of line in going into hiding, and doing everything on her own. 'You should have come to us with your suspicions right at the start,' they'd said. 'This really wasn't the best way to go about things.'

She'd become quite angry at that. 'How was I to know who to go to? Even my father's best friend was a traitor!'

*Yes, but still, Miss Marcel, somehow you shouldn't have been so* unladylike . . .

And then of course, there was the guilt she would have to live with, that her information had caused the deaths of four men. The papers had gone over and over the details: the earlier editions – before the whole story was known – concentrating on the tragic widows left behind, the driver who'd also been gunned down; and there was no way Livvy could ever talk herself out of feeling guilt for that! The machine guns were Mongolian LDK 42s – and it was suspected that the unfriendly Mongolian government had long been training anti-Roman guerrilla movements and supplying them with weapons. Livvy hoped she'd had her last encounter with the *Bleiddiaid*, even though it was due to them that she had escaped.

But she couldn't get the thought out of her head that momentous changes were afoot, and that she could never have gone back to that old safe life, the violin lessons, her friends at Sixth Precinct, Max . . .

One day, she'd light a candle for Max and make an offering at Minerva's temple, but she wasn't going to do it under Diana Cato's hard blue gaze, no way . . .

While she was thinking this, the door opened without

so much as a warning knock, and in came Iris, wearing her street clothes.

'Get your coat on, please, miss,' she said. 'Madam says we're to go to Astra's to get fitted up for your school uniform.'

# 33

She hadn't been to Astra's, the department store in the city centre, since her sticky meeting with Cai, and the thought of being fitted up for school uniform filled her with dread. Still, it was an outing, and even an outing with stiff-backed, disapproving Iris was better than no outing at all. She wore her new winter coat and a pink hat and gloves that reminded her of the poor girl who'd been snatched off the bus (another guilty memory that she would have to live with). She had money with her to pay for the school uniform and a little pocket money too, though she couldn't think of anything she'd fancy at the moment.

Iris walked briskly by her side, hardly saying anything. She'd been with the family since she was a girl, and really, her stiff gait seemed to say, she deserved better than *this!*

Astra's was a big store, three storeys high, and boasted the first plate-glass windows to be seen in Wroxeter. They went through heavy mahogany doors, onto soft Indian carpets, and peachy lighting. The counters by the door on the ground floor held cosmetics, and smells of jasmine and musk drifted everywhere. Iris walked past with her head held high.

A big curving mahogany staircase led up to the first floor (women's wear, lingerie, girls' wear, schoolwear) and they were just about to go up, when a voice called Iris's name. She greeted a friend delightedly, another servant, judging by her neat navy-blue coat, and at once the two launched into an exchange of news and greetings, ignoring Livvy. Livvy picked up that there had been some sort of scandal at the other woman's house involving Madam and the children's tutor. Livvy listened for a while, and then edged gradually away.

At the cosmetic counter, she sprayed herself with something that smelled of old ladies and fur coats. Ugh. The over made-up woman behind the counter tried to interest her in a twin pack – perfume and hand-cream – but soon gave up. Out of the corner of her eye, Livvy could see the two women, still talking. Iris was still not looking in her direction. Livvy inched further and further down the counter, fiddling with perfume sprays. 'You really can't smell them, madam, if you put so many on,' sniffed the assistant. 'We recommend trying only one or two at a time.' By this time, Livvy had moved close to the door and the woman behind the counter had turned away to tidy the shelves.

She shot another look at Iris and her friend. The scandal of Madam's doings still occupied them – neither looked at her. She made her mind up in an instant, sauntered over to the entrance, threw one last look at them to check – and then slipped out through the doors into the street.

Now she began to walk briskly past the famous plate-glass windows, with their array of the latest spring clothes – all pinks and lilacs and soft greens. Livvy had

215

a strange feeling that somehow this was never going to be for her, never again. She quickened her pace now, and tried to think about outwitting pursuers – something she'd got quite good at. She slipped into a busy stationers that she knew had a back exit into another street, and from there, turned sharply away down a quiet street of office blocks.

She quickly made her way through the city centre, nipping sharply across roads, avoiding hooves and wheels, across squares where office lads ate sandwiches, and hopeful pigeons strutted, through smaller streets of local shops, greengrocers, butchers, dairies, past men and boys cat-calling and whistling – something Glyn Howells hadn't come in for a lot of – yes, that was one thing she'd have to get used to as a girl again – through estates of workers' houses, through schools and factories, bathhouses, dogtracks and temples, the streets getting narrower and scruffier as she went.

The smell of all-day breakfast filled the air – and here was the Black Dragon. Don's flat was over there somewhere. She walked on briskly, down to the docks.

They were busy this morning; a couple of large freight steamers had just docked, and men carried out heavy bundles. Barges bobbed on the grey water, and waves slapped against wooden sides. The smell of steam and oil and rotting vegetation filled the air; screaming seagulls wheeled and dived around her.

But no sign of the *Diligence*. She asked a couple of seamen, but nobody seemed to know. One of them offered her sex. She blushed and went on. Finally one older man said, no, he didn't know, hadn't seen her for a couple of weeks.

Disconcerted, she hurried away. Maybe Cai would

be at home. So she traced her way through the little smoky terraces, until she found his street and knocked on the door of his house. Her earlier excitement had given way to anxiety, as though some terrible upheaval awaited her.

She knocked on the door. For a long time nothing happened, then she could hear footsteps. The door opened slowly, and Cai's mother stood there, wiping floury hands on her apron. It took her a few seconds to recognise Livvy and, when she did, her tone was not enthusiastic. 'You've got proper clothes on at last,' was all she said.

'Please, Mrs Llewelyn, I have to see Cai.'

'Oh, you have to, do you? Well, he isn't here.'

'Where is he, please?'

'You've given my family enough trouble,' she said. 'Why should I tell you?'

And she made as if to shut the door. Livvy managed to get her foot in the gap. 'Listen,' she said. 'I know you don't like me, but I'm really fond of Cai. And I've run away from my chaperone to see him. I'm going to be in huge trouble anyway when I go back, so please let me be in trouble for a good reason.'

Cai's mother stood back in the doorway, and eyed her up and down. Her dark eyes looked like Cai's, without the laughter. 'Dry dock,' she said eventually. 'Boat's being repaired. They're all there, Cai and his dad. Down this road, turn left, then right, through the big gates . . .'

She could hear the clang of hammers as she approached the dry dock. Half a dozen small boats were there, at different angles, while keels and hulls and planking were repaired. A strong smell of tar drifted over; Cai sat on the deck of the beached *Diligence,* listlessly slapping on something black and sticky.

She'd approached quietly, and he hadn't heard her.

'Hello, Cai,' she said.

He looked up, stared a moment, and then put his wet brush down. In a second, he was over the deck and by her side. 'Well,' he said. 'Look what's turned up.'

'Are you pleased to see me?' she said, a little uncertainly.

'You bet I am,' he said, and took her in his arms and kissed her.

Somebody wolf-whistled, and he laughed and pushed her gently away. 'Nosy lot,' he said. 'You look good, Glyn Howells.'

'So do you.'

He laughed. 'I look crap. Covered in tar and filth. Old man's off to the pub, leaving me to do the dirty work. Well, sod it. Come on.'

'Where are we going?'

'Anywhere. Just to walk. There's so much I want to know about you.'

'There's so much I have to tell you.'

'How did you get away from the dragon?'

'It was the dragon's assistant. I left her in Astra's.'

'And are you all right?'

'Well, yes. Bored.'

'Me too.'

They linked arms, and he steered her onto the path that ran alongside the canal, down to the docks one way, and following the canal into the country on the other.

'But you've been all right, really?'

'Yes,' she said. 'But it's all so odd, so different. Cai, I'm sure something is happening. Everything's changing.'

'Yes,' he said, 'I feel that too. Things can't go back to what they were. But will they get better or worse?'

'I almost don't care,' she said. 'I just don't want to go back.'

He looked down at her, oddly. 'You say you ran away from the dragon?'

'Yes.'

'So you're in trouble, I reckon.'

'Big trouble.'

He kissed her on the forehead. 'Bad girl.' Then he pulled away and looked at her. 'Can't get used to you as a girl. I think I like it. Maybe when the hair grows back. Not sure about pink, though.'

'Present from the dragon.'

'Hmm,' he said. Then, 'See that funnel over there? That's the northwest ferry. Leaves in an hour. Goes all the way to Chester, then round the Cymric shore. Fetches up in the Isle of Môn. We could be there in a day.'

'What about papers?'

'I've got a waterways permit. Get me to Cymru, anyhow. Then it doesn't matter. What about you?'

'Well, I've got my family identity card.' She had taken it to Astra's to get a discount on her school uniform. She opened her purse and showed him the card and her money. He grinned and shook out a few coins from his own pocket.

'We're rich,' he said. 'Do well in Cymru, we would.'

'What would we do there?'

'Well, first maybe we'd call in on my cousins. Then I'd look for work. Maybe on the fishing boats.'

'You could play your guitar round the pubs. You're so good, they'd pay to hear you.'

'You could learn too, with all those posh violin lessons behind you. Can you sing?'

'Yes, a bit. In tune, anyway.'

'There you go,' he said. 'We'd be dynamite. My playing and your looks. They'd be gagging for us.'

'Speak Cymric, do you?'

'A bit,' he said. 'Ma speaks it. Says things when she doesn't want Dad to hear. Which is fairly often.'

'My grandmother spoke it,' said Livvy softly, remembering Nain, and the slow, comfortable afternoons in the big gloomy flat. 'I could probably still say *hello* and *goodbye*, and *isn't the weather nice.*'

'Girl of many talents.'

'All about to be squashed in my bloody new school,' she said bitterly.

'When do you start?'

'I was supposed to be measured up for the uniform today,' she said, 'when I did a bunk.' Then she stopped. 'Cai?'

'What?'

'When you said about the ferry? Were you serious?'

He was quiet for a while. Then he said, 'Yes. Yes, I was as it happens. What about you?'

She thought. A ticking-off from Diana Cato, followed by another one in a few weeks from Tony. Her mother needed someone to look after her, but she'd never let Livvy get close, and Tony would probably be more efficient anyway. The garden, her father's garden and the statue of Minerva, the family house, they'd never be the same to her. Max gone, Sixth Precinct closed, Don dismissed . . . nothing was ever going to be like it had been. But . . .

'The past . . .' she said, 'it's kind of hard to get away from.'

'Maybe,' he said. 'But it's gone anyway, whether you want it or not.'

'Yes,' she mused. 'And you know, apart from a few things that I can't get back anyway, I don't think I'll miss it, any of it.'

'So think about the future, then.'

The northwest ferry boomed in the distance. In the sound were wild mountains and waterfalls, and rocky shores and silent deep valleys, distances she couldn't imagine. There was freedom, and a life that was made up of her own choices, not the choices that others were making for her. There'd be hardships too – you couldn't avoid those – but she was strong now, she knew that, and maybe she could cope with them, especially if Cai was with her. Cai was right. The past had gone. Now came the future. They were the future.

She pretended to hesitate, but really the decision was made in a split second. He looked at her, anxiously, as if he'd said too much, and wondered if he'd upset her.

'Yes,' she said. 'You're right. I can't go back.'

'Would you come with me, if I got on that ferry?'

'Yes,' she said.

'Sure?'

'Quite.'

'No second thoughts?'

'None.'

The ferry boomed again, more urgently now. She could see last-minute passengers running along the quaysides. Yes, she had never felt more sure of anything in her life.

'Then let's go,' he said with one of his sudden smiles. *'Ti'n barod?'*

And then all at once she could feel the words coming back to her, out of a past she barely knew she had, but one that was suddenly about to become her future. *'Ydw, dw i'n barod,'* she said. 'I'm ready.'